EMER

CW00384890

Staff Nurse Laurel Swann—nicknamed Laurel the
Unflappable—finds it hard to live up to her name
after she has met Bruce Tyson, the dynamic surgeon
in the Accident and Emergency Department.

*Books you will enjoy
in our Doctor–Nurse series*

FLYAWAY SISTER by Lisa Cooper
TROPICAL NURSE by Margaret Barker
LADY IN HARLEY STREET by Anne Vinton
FIRST-YEAR'S FANCY by Lynne Collins
DESERT FLOWER by Dana James
INDIAN OCEAN DOCTORS by Juliet Shore
CRUISE NURSE by Clare Lavenham
CAPTIVE HEART by Hazel Fisher
A PROFESSIONAL SECRET by Kate Norway
NURSE ON CALL by Leonie Craig
THE GILDED CAGE by Sarah Franklin
A SURGEON CALLED AMANDA by Elizabeth Harrison
VICTORY FOR VICTORIA by Betty Neels
SHAMROCK NURSE by Elspeth O'Brien
ICE VENTURE NURSE by Lydia Balmain
TREAD SOFTLY, NURSE by Lynne Collins
DR VENABLES' PRACTICE by Anne Vinton
NURSE OVERBOARD by Meg Wisgate
DOCTORS IN DISPUTE by Jean Evans
WRONG DOCTOR JOHN by Kate Starr

EMERGENCY NURSE

BY

GRACE READ

MILLS & BOON LIMITED
London · Sydney · Toronto

First published in Great Britain 1983
by Mills & Boon Limited, 15–16 Brook's Mews,
London W1A 1DR

Australian copyright 1983
Philippine copyright 1983

ISBN 0 263 74379 9

Set in 11 on 12 pt Linotron Times
03/0883

Photoset by Rowland Phototypesetting Ltd
Bury St Edmunds, Suffolk
Made and printed in Great Britain by
Richard Clay (The Chaucer Press) Ltd
Bungay, Suffolk

For Margaret

CHAPTER ONE

THAT April Saturday the Accident and Emergency Department of the old Riversdale Hospital on the outskirts of London had seen more than its usual quota of drunks and football hooligans. Staff Nurse Laurel Swann rested one aching foot on the other as she waited for the casualty officer, freckle-faced Andy Logan, to finish scrubbing his hands before treating the patient on the bed.

'We're going to put a few stitches in that gash over your eye,' Andy said briskly to the nervous, long-haired youth who had been a victim of a pub brawl.

The lad looked apprehensive. 'Don't I get put to sleep first?'

'Oh, we'll give you a local, son,' said Andy reassuringly. 'Don't worry, you won't feel anything.'

Opening up a sterile suture pack, Laurel handed surgical gloves to the doctor. While he eased them on to his hands she broke off the top of an ampoule of Lignocaine and held it for him to draw up into the syringe.

'This is the same stuff you get at the dentist's when you have a tooth out,' Andy explained, cleaning the wound and surrounding area with antiseptic lotion before injecting the drug.

'Just a couple of pricks.' Laurel took the patient's

hand. 'There, that wasn't too bad, was it?'

The tense youth relaxed, gave a feeble grin, but kept a tight grip on her fingers. 'It's not your face, matey.'

She curbed a smile. 'Well, you'll have to let go of me so that we can get on with the job.' She reached for a dressing in readiness to cover the wound after suturing. 'He's won prizes for needlework,' she joked with the boy. 'You'll hardly see the scar when the stitches come out.'

Andy struck a pose of mock astonishment. 'Since when did you join my fan club, Laurel?'

She patted a careless yawn. 'Don't let it go to your head. I always give credit where it's due.'

He grinned and after satisfying himself that the affected area was well numbed, proceeded to close the gaping cut with neat stitches. Laurel snipped the ends as he tied. 'There you are,' said Andy when he finished. 'Come back and see us in five days' time.' Stripping off the gloves he sauntered back to the doctors' office to await his next case.

Laurel put the sterile dressing in place over the wound, saw the boy on his way and cleared up the treatment room.

Going back to the reception area in search of the next person requiring attention, she was almost run down by a couple of louts larking about with wheel-chairs in the corridor.

'What are you doing?' Laurel asked.

'Waiting for our mate,' said one. 'He's getting 'is wrist plastered.'

'Well, kindly put those chairs back where you found them and wait quietly, will you?'

'Right miss, yes miss,' returned the other, jumping to attention with an insolent leer.

They turned and raced back with the chairs in the opposite direction.

Laurel went on to find the next patient, a small girl of six accompanied by her mother. The woman held out the child's hand to show a minor slit on her middle finger. 'Her rabbit bit it,' she explained.

'Oh! Well, that doesn't look too bad . . . but I'll get a doctor to see it.'

Andy Logan was engaged with another patient, but Laurel found Dr Moira Carp free. The exquisite Moira, tall, willowy and expensively groomed, turned down the corners of her shapely mouth. 'A rabbit bite?' she said with bored indifference. 'I suppose I'd better look at it.'

Laurel followed the doctor to the examination room, admiring the girl's softly swinging blonde hair. Her own hair was curly and wayward and an in-between sort of brown. She wished she had a few more inches, like Moira. You could hardly be called statuesque when you were barely five-foot-two.

Dr Carp took the child's hand and inspected it. 'Hardly anything at all, is it?' she said with a languid glance towards the mother, her manner clearly suggesting they were wasting her time. 'Has she had her pre-school injections?'

'Oh yes, Doctor. She's had everything like that.'

'So she'll be covered for tetanus. Nurse will see to the cut for you. A couple of steri-strips should do it,' she drawled, turning to Laurel.

At the sound of rushing feet and coarse laughter from outside Moira paused in mild curiosity. 'Good gracious, Staff, whatever is that commotion?'

Laurel groaned and raised her eyebrows. 'There's a couple of hooligans out there fooling around with the wheelchairs. I've warned them off once . . .' She stormed outside, green eyes flashing, and placed her slight figure in the path of the rowdies. 'Get out, you! This is a hospital, not a skid patch. Go on . . . GET OUT. And take those chairs back where they came from.'

Small though she was, at the authority in her voice the culprits subsided. Sheepishly they wheeled the chairs back to the reception area and slunk into a corner to await their pal.

'Blimey!' chuckled one of the porters as he wheeled an empty trolley back to base, 'That made 'em sit up, didn't it, ducks?'

Laurel grinned self-consciously and went back to attend to her small patient. Taking the child to the treatment room, she cleaned the cut with Savlon solution before pulling the edges together with steri-strips and placing a plaster over it.

'There you are, love. That should heal up all right. No, there'll be no need for her to be seen again,' she said in answer to the mother's query.

It was approaching seven o'clock and the rush of patients had petered out for the moment. Sister Maguire, going off-duty at four-thirty, had handed the emergency bleeper over to Laurel. Now, as she tidied up the treatment area, the undulating sound of the bleep came from her pocket. A red alert? *Oh God! That's all I need*, she thought, making for the office to ring the Central Ambulance Station for details.

'Riversdale A and E,' she announced when they answered.

'Hallo Riversdale, we've got a multiple RTA for you. Three stretcher cases coming in about five minutes . . . one a male with severe head injuries, okay?'

'Right,' said Laurel, and she hurried to alert the rest of the team.

When the ambulances began to arrive the whole of the department was geared to intensive activity. Staff were stretched to capacity, with orthopaedic, surgical and neurological registrars having to be consulted.

With Louise Bates, a second-year student, to assist her, Laurel received the unconscious youth with head injuries. The ambulance team had already inserted an airway to assist his breathing.

'Came off his motorbike,' they told her, transferring the boy to a hospital trolley. 'The police are getting in touch with the family.'

With speed being vital in the case of head injuries, the casualty was hurried through to the resuscitation room. Laurel and Louise began carefully removing his clothing. Andy Logan arrived. 'Newman is on his way,' he reported. 'We'd better get on with putting up a drip.'

Blood was sent for cross-matching and the mobile X-ray unit summoned to take pictures of the damage. The films were rushed through and were ready for the neuro-surgeon to screen when he came. Together the doctors studied the X-rays, locating the fracture site.

'Right . . . just put a sterile dressing over the head-wound for now,' ordered Mr Newman, 'and we'll get him straight to theatre.'

After attending to the details, Laurel called for a porter to assist her in transferring the boy to theatre along with his notes.

Her spell of duty was almost up by the time she returned to the department. Making for the office, she bumped into Louise who burst from a minor-ops theatre in tears.

'What's wrong?' Laurel asked.

'H-he wants someone else,' sobbed Louise. 'I cut my finger breaking open an ampoule . . . a-and then I went and dropped the sterile pack . . .'

Laurel frowned. 'Who is it?'

'Mr Tyson,' gulped Louise.

'Okay . . . you go and calm down. I'll see to him.' She marched into the room prepared for fireworks with the senior surgical registrar.

Bruce Tyson was a large man, his very size intimidating. Holding gloved hands aloft ready to suture the badly lacerated leg of a teenage girl, he was talking quietly to the patient. He glanced towards Laurel as she entered, giving her a cool, appraising stare from deep-set, piercingly blue eyes. His dark brows narrowed. 'Not *another* accident-prone nurse,' he growled.

The remark surprised her because, although she had seen him about the hospital, she had never personally been called upon to work with him before. There was, admittedly, a strange feeling she had experienced, that she had come across him somewhere, sometime. That well-shaped head with its thatch of shiny dark waves curling attractively into his strong neck, the firm jaw-line and the lean cheeks, had left an impression on her from some previous occasion. She couldn't recall where. There was a healthy outdoor glow about the man. She could picture him taking a mighty swing at a golf ball, or in the middle of a rugby scrum, like her boyfriend, Gary.

Laurel drew a steadying breath and said with more composure than she felt, 'Can I help you, sir?'

He nodded curtly towards the scattered suture pack on the floor. 'Do you think you can open one of those for me without dropping it?'

'Certainly.' She stepped to the cabinet, took out a fresh sterile suture pack, ripped off the outer covering and held it for him to take the things he needed.

'Thank you. I suppose gold medals do count for something after all,' he observed tartly.

She was even more surprised. How did he know she had been a gold medallist at her training school? It wasn't something she talked about.

Maintaining a prudent silence, Laurel cut off the silk as he tied a stitch. She looked towards the slightly nervous patient and gave her a discreet wink.

'And can you wink the other eye, Nurse?' queried Tyson, without looking up from his suturing.

'Oh yes, I'm very versatile,' she returned sweetly.

'At least you don't dissolve into tears the moment I open my mouth.'

She snipped another stitch as he tied it. 'If you harass people you can't expect them to perform well.'

He straightened up and fixed her with a chilling glare. 'I thought Casualty staff were meant to be on the ball. All I ask for is efficiency. What's the use of some half-baked junior who can't cope?'

'Everyone has to learn,' said Laurel, unperturbed. 'Why are you doing this little job anyway?'

'If you really require an explanation, the department seemed to be stretched and this young lady looked in need of attention.' He turned a more kindly face towards the patient and softened his voice. 'Is it quite comfortable, Wendy?'

The girl gave a shy smile. She had been listening with mild amusement to the cut and thrust between Laurel and the registrar. 'Yes, I'm fine, thank you,' she said.

'Good! It's nearly finished.' He carried on closing the wound with Laurel snipping expertly as he tied. 'I gather I'm not harassing you,' he said, shooting Laurel a penetrating glance from beneath his brows.

'Me? Good heavens, no! Laurel the unflappable they call me,' she returned flippantly.

He grunted and finished his work. 'Well, Miss Unflappable, can I safely leave you to put a sterile dressing and tubi-gauze covering over that?'

She saluted smartly. 'Yes, sir! I take it she can go home then?'

'Of course. Come back in a week for removal of

stitches, that's the drill, isn't it?' He stripped off his gloves, turned a devastating smile on the patient and walked away.

Laurel finished off the dressing, chatting to the girl in a friendly manner. 'His bark's worse than his bite. You had the top brass there, love. He usually only does major surgery in main theatres.'

Wendy gave a tremulous laugh. 'Ooh! I thought he was absolutely gorgeous.'

'Mmm . . . I suppose he is rather dishy, if you like the strong, silent type.' Laurel helped the girl into a wheelchair. 'I'd better get some transport laid on for you. You may have to hang about a bit . . . but we'll find you a cup of tea while you're waiting.'

Wheeling her charge along to the reception area she came across Louise, now in control of herself.

'Did you get on all right, Laurel?'

'Yes, fine. No problems.'

'Thanks for helping me out.' Louise made a doleful face. 'It was nicking my finger that did it. And I've never done that before on an ampoule. I got the willies, having to work with Tyson.'

'Oh, he's a bit pompous,' allowed Laurel. 'Illusions of grandeur, I shouldn't wonder. But don't let it throw you. Would you like to get Wendy a cup of tea?'

'Sure,' said Louise with a grateful smile.

Laurel went back to clear up before going off duty, preoccupied with thoughts of the taciturn registrar. In spite of her assumed indifference, she did know what Louise meant about Bruce Tyson. She too had felt the undercurrent of power about the man. Usually her experience in dealing with the medical hierarchy prevented her being overawed. But she had to admit that there was something about Mr Tyson that made her legs feel weak.

The night staff had by now put in an appearance and most of the day shift were on their way home, Staff Nurses Kathie Moran and Mollie O'Brien among them.

'We're going for a drink, Laurel. Coming?' called Kathie.

'No, not tonight, thanks. I'm not quite ready.'

Five minutes later, going along to the office to hand over the emergency bleep to Night Sister, Laurel found the small room crowded with staff.

Andy Logan lolled in a chair with his feet on the wastepaper bin, his sandy hair flopping over one eye.

'Excuse me,' Laurel said, reaching past him to pick up her hold-all from the floor.

'You doing anything interesting tonight?' He jerked her cap forward over her eyes.

With an indulgent sigh she took it off and stuffed it into her bag. 'It's a bath and bed for me—if you call that interesting.'

He grinned. 'Could be . . . if you had company. Pity I can't join you. Think of me still slogging away here while you're wallowing.'

She wrinkled her pert nose at him. 'You bring tears to my eyes,' she said, putting on her raincoat and turning up the collar. 'Goodnight all . . . have fun.'

But stepping out towards the exit, she did sympathise with the hardworking doctors who often put in long hours of duty with few breaks. No one in any other walk of life would put up with such conditions, she reflected.

Pushing through the swing-doors she breathed deeply of the rain-washed night air, refreshing after the centrally-heated atmosphere of the hospital. Home now to the furnished house which she shared with Dilys and Emma, and a nice long soak before going to bed. What a way to spend Saturday night!

Briefly she wondered what her boyfriend, Gary, was doing. He'd have been playing rugger that afternoon. There'd probably be the usual social at the clubhouse, plenty of girls to chat up. She sighed. It was a situation she had become used to. She could hardly expect him to be a plaster saint since they were so many miles apart and her weekends were at a premium.

Laurel's home was beyond Sevenoaks. Her father, Dr Swann, shared a thriving practice there with Gary's father, Dr Grantham.

Gary and she had more or less grown up together, but he had not chosen to follow his father into medicine. He had opted for law and was now with a firm of solicitors.

Although there had been a kind of understanding between them since adolescent days, they had never actually got around to talking about marriage. Gary had once asked her, rather grumpily, why she didn't give up this nursing lark and come back home to look after her father. Then they would be able to see more of each other.

'Oh, Dad doesn't need me,' Laurel had said, 'he's got his housekeeper . . . and Ingrid Spelen.'

'Well, it's no good you getting jealous of her,'

Gary had countered. 'You can't expect a present-able chap like your father to remain celibate at his age.'

She had been indignant at his accusation, but deep down she knew she did rather resent her father's girlfriend. Laurel's mother had died when she was seventeen. She had never quite got over the loss. It seemed to her that if you loved someone very much they either died or went away. Her elder brother, Tom, whom she adored, had gone away; first to school and later to university. They had never been quite as close since and now he spent most of his time abroad. No, it was best not to get too fond of people, she had decided. That way you could not get hurt.

Going over to the car park, she found that some careless driver had evidently reversed into her Mini and smashed one of her rear lights. 'Hell's bells! The end of a perfect day!' she muttered in annoyance.

She flung her things into the back of the car and drove the circuitous route towards the hospital gates. On the way, out of the corner of her eye she glimpsed the white-coated figure of Bruce Tyson striding in the direction of the residents' quarters. He was not alone. Clinging to his arm, looking up at him in a decidedly coy manner, was the elegant Moira Carp.

That man was too handsome for any woman's peace of mind, Laurel mused. The long, lithe limbs had a sensual grace which sent delicious shivers down her own spine. His broad-shouldered, deep-chested physique suggested disciplined power and authority, and those startlingly blue deep-set eyes seemed to bore right through to one's innermost thoughts.

And however had he known about her gold medal? Her thoughts sped back to Presentation Day at the Royal Heathside in her final year there. 'Another accident-prone nurse,' he had said. Suddenly, with a flash of distant memory, it came to her. After bobbing her curtsey to the royal personage who had pinned on her medal, she had tripped going down the platform steps. But for that stalwart figure who had leapt from his seat in the front row to catch her, she would have gone sprawling.

She could still recall the fleeting impression of his solid strength when he had come to her assistance. She had caught a brief glimpse of him later, at the informal tea for relatives, but they did not come into contact and she had never known who he was.

Reaching the house, Laurel pulled into the drive, garaged the car and let herself in. There was no one else at home. Emma, doing her course on neuro-surgical, was on nights. Dilys, a physiotherapist, had left a note on the hall table saying she'd gone to a farewell party for one of her team. It was in the doctors' mess, and Laurel could come on if she liked.

Laurel decided she was too tired and not really in the mood for party going. Dumping her gear in her bedroom, she kicked off her duty shoes, stuffed her crumpled white uniform in the linen-bin and put on her brown velour dressing-gown. Then she went down to the kitchen to make herself a much-needed cup of coffee.

On the kitchen cabinet was some post for her. One letter was from a girl she had trained with, and the other envelope was addressed in Gary's scrawl. He usually telephoned . . . hardly ever wrote. Curious, she opened Gary's letter first. The contents hit her like a blow to the solar plexus.

'My dear Laurie,' Gary wrote, 'I hate having to do this, but I'd rather you heard from me than from someone else. The truth is, sweetie, I think I've met my soul-mate. You must admit you haven't made yourself very available lately. Our romance has grown a bit stale, hasn't it? Perhaps we know each other too well. Anyway, you're such a pet I know it won't be long before some other lucky guy snaps you up. We can still be friends, I hope. And if ever you need any legal advice, you can count on me! Sorry, love. Be happy. Yours as ever, Gary.'

Laurel put the letter down and stared into space, feeling stunned. She supposed she ought to cry or something, but oddly enough she didn't feel tearful. Instead, apart from the blow to her pride and the indignity of being ditched, she discovered that her main reaction was a kind of relief that it was over and that he'd been big enough to tell her so. And it proved that she had been right, didn't it, not to give her heart unreservedly? If you let yourself love people too much they either went away or something else happened to them. All the same, it was ego-shattering to have been dumped so unceremoniously.

With a heavy sigh Laurel opened her other letter. It was a wedding invitation, which only served to highlight her own rejection.

Going to run her bath, she made an effort to push all dismal thoughts to the back of her mind and concentrate on immediate matters, like her damaged car. Tomorrow she would have to put it into the garage to get that rear light fixed.

But it was not the end of her long-time romance that would insist on pushing to the forefront of her mind, it was the keen-eyed countenance of the senior surgical registrar. She wondered what he had been doing at the Royal Heathside on Presentation Day. Of course, doctors were a floating population, going from one appointment to another in the course of their progress, so perhaps it wasn't surprising.

At least today she had been able to prove to him that she wasn't the accident-prone type he had seemed to have labelled her.

Luxuriating in her scented bath, Laurel fell to wondering if Bruce Tyson were married. He did seem more mature than some of the medics, so he probably was. What would it be like to be married to a man like that? She could imagine he would be very masterful. Of course there were girls who liked the macho-type, Laurel reflected, but she was not one of them. She believed in equality.

All the same, there was a certain rock-like aura about the registrar which would make him a very comforting person to have on your side if you were in trouble, she thought.

CHAPTER TWO

EARLY on Sunday morning Laurel's alarm awoke her from a troubled sleep. The dream was still vividly clear in her mind. She lay for a moment in a welter of relief, her heart beating a tattoo. Thank God it had been a dream and not reality . . . that look of disdain on Bruce Tyson's face as she scurried around in some hazy hospital setting, continually dropping the things he asked for, while the glamorous Moira Carp looked on with contemptuous amusement.

At first sleep had proved elusive, her mind overactive with the events of the day. She had heard Dilys come home in the small hours. When she did eventually drop off, it was only to find herself in that awful nightmare situation.

How silly she was, letting the man affect her like that. Laurel smiled at her own stupidity. She was as good as any nurse in the department—better than some. She would not allow herself to be intimidated by the imperious Bruce Tyson.

With a firm resolve never to be browbeaten by high-and-mighty surgeons, she jumped out of bed and went to the bathroom to wash. Going downstairs afterwards to make coffee, she carried it back to her room to drink while dressing.

Dilys drifted into her bedroom, flopping on the bed and yawning hugely. 'Hi, Laurel! You missed a good party last night.' She ran her fingers through her dark, urchin haircut. 'It was great.'

'Oh, I was dead on my feet,' said Laurel, fastening the silver-buckled navy belt around her trim waist. 'Besides which, I was in a mood . . . had a ding-dong with Bruce Tyson.'

'Did you? What about?'

Laurel tugged a comb through her unruly, nut-brown curls. 'He had one of the second-years in tears, the wretch, and he had a go at me as well, so I gave him as good as I got.'

Dilys grinned. 'Wish I'd been a fly on the wall.'

'If you'd been a fly on the wall he'd probably have swatted you. He was in that frame of mind!'

'Oh well, all part of life's rich pattern. My day off, thank goodness. I'm going back to bed.' Dilys yawned again and trailed back to her room.

Finishing her coffee, Laurel put on her raincoat, picked up her hold-all and set off for work. There was a mildness in the air but a thick ground mist rising after yesterday's rain. Getting out the car, she switched on her sidelights and drove with care through the haze. Presently the ancient jumble of buildings which comprised the Riversdale Hospital loomed into view. She turned in through the large iron gates, giving a cheery wave to the lodge-keeper in passing.

What a hotch-potch of styles the place was, she thought, viewing the buildings with a cross between love and loathing. The Riversdale had first started out as a cottage hospital in Victorian times. It had grown over the years and now housed a complete range of departments and services. The various additions were connected by covered ways, which could prove very draughty for patients being taken to X-ray or being transferred from one place to another.

It was a far cry from that modern complex the Royal Heathside, where Laurel had trained, but she knew the work done was of an equally high standard despite the more humble conditions. Wards were of the 'Nightingale' variety, long rooms with beds on either side, screened by floral curtains, each with a couple of sidewards for very ill patients. The Path Lab was housed in a separate pre-fab type of building. Behind the hospital were purpose-built residents' quarters and the Nurses' Home. The Accident and Emergency Unit, in which direction Laurel now headed, was the most recently up-dated part of the hospital.

At that hour of the morning there was no difficulty in finding a parking spot. After depositing her things in the staff room and fastening her frilled cap in place with white hairclips, Laurel made for Sister's office where everyone was gathering to hear the night report.

'The usual Saturday night story,' Sister Dustin told them, 'and why people leave it to the weekend to get worried about their constipation I can't imagine!' She ran her finger down the report book. 'We must have seen nearly thirty patients. One cardiac arrest died on us . . . his next-of-kin will be coming to identify the body. Three chest pains . . . they went to Coronary Care. A diabetic coma and an RTA with compound fracture of tib and fib and crushed ribs . . . she went to Orthopaedics. We

haven't been able to contact the parents yet . . .
you'll have to keep trying. The usual hypochon-
driacs and drunks. It was three a.m. before we
cleared. All you've got left now is our old regular,
Charlie Broome. He's sleeping off his meths beano
in Room Three.'

Sister Dustin donned her cloak, said cheerio and
left the day staff to it.

The department was of necessity mainly manned
by well-qualified staff, all capable of making rapid
decisions in times of crisis. But there were always
some student nurses doing their stint in the course
of their general training.

This morning, besides Sister Maguire, there
were four staff nurses as well as two post-grads (one
of which was Laurel) taking the A and E course as
an extra qualification. All were allocated tasks.
Laurel was given the minor-ops theatres to look
after. 'And take Rosemary under your wing, will
you, dear?' said Sister Maguire in a motherly manner. 'It's her first experience of A and E.'

Inwardly Laurel groaned, but she smiled encouragingly at the lanky eighteen-year-old, remembering her own student days before confidence
built up. The girl was obviously nervous, constantly
fidgeting with her paper cap which seemed disin-
clined to stay put on her floppy fair hair.

'Come on then, Rosemary,' Laurel said brightly,
'It's all hands to cleaning at this time of the morning.'

Going along to Theatre One, she set the girl to
cleaning the surfaces of trolleys and other equipment with Dispray. She herself checked and stock-

ed up on the supply of sterile packs, dressings and drugs, oxygen and suction apparatus and i.v. fluid packs.

'I've finished that, Staff. What shall I do now?' came Rosemary's little-girl voice behind her.

'You have?' Laurel glanced around. 'Yes, that all looks fine. Well, er . . . I'll go over the Boyle's machine with you now.'

'What's that, Staff?'

'The anaesthetics trolley,' Laurel explained, and she went over in detail the workings of the machine and the equipment needed to put a patient under a general anaesthetic.

Rosemary looked at her in admiration. 'Gosh! It's so complicated . . . I shall never remember all that.'

'Oh yes, you will in time. It's surprising how much you absorb without realising it.'

When Laurel was satisfied that everything was as it should be, they went on to check on Theatre Two.

Their routine work was completed without interruption, Sunday morning being a customary respite after the Saturday night rush. Laurel took her protégé along to the coffee room, where most of the staff were assembled for a quick refresher before patients began to drift in.

'Charlie seems to have got himself together now,' Sister Maguire said. 'How about giving him a bath, Laurel, before we get busy?'

'Okay, Sister.' Laurel grinned. 'He's going to love me! Have we got any fresh clothes anywhere? It's not much use giving him a bath and putting those dirty rags back on.'

'I'll ring the Day Centre and get some sent over,' promised Sister.

'Size nine shoes, if I remember.' Laurel finished her coffee and jumped up to go in search of the tramp. 'Better get on with it, I suppose. Who wants to help me?'

'Can I, Staff?' piped up Rosemary, eagerly.

'Okay, you find a wheelchair and bring it along.' Laurel went off in the direction of Room Three with Rosemary following close on her heels like a puppy who'd been patted.

The tramp was still slumped on the bed with his eyes closed, but he was no longer in a stupor. 'Good morning, Mr Broome,' Laurel said briskly, 'We're going to give you a nice bath and clean you up a bit.'

Charlie opened bleary blue eyes to peer at her. 'You again, is it?' he growled. 'My deah young lady . . . I don't wanna bath. All I want is some grub. Just you gimme some breakfast and I'll push off.'

'Oh, come on, Mr Broome, you know you'll feel much better for a tub,' Laurel coaxed as Rosemary arrived with the wheelchair. 'Sit yourself in here and we'll find you a change of clothes to smarten you up a bit . . . size nine shoes, isn't it?'

Muttering expletives under his breath, the smelly, bearded, grey-haired tramp heaved himself off the bed and into the chair. 'Bits of chits of girls ordering me about,' he grumbled, looking like an affronted turkey-cock. 'I'm old enough to be your grandfather, you know? They ought to've taken me to the nick. The fuzz give a chap a good meal . . . not all this bother with *baths*.'

Laurel grinned at Rosemary as they pushed him along to the bathroom, ignoring his protests. Helping him off with his filthy clothes and gaping shoes, they bundled the lot into a plastic bag for burning. Rosemary went for the clean clothes which Sister Maguire had obtained from the supply donated by the Friends of Riversdale for people in need. Soon a much sweeter-smelling Charlie was tucking into his breakfast of sausage, bacon and baked beans from the hospital kitchen.

Other casualties started arriving and the waiting-room began to fill up. With doctors' surgeries being closed, people with even trivial problems were apt to run to the A and E department with their weekend worries.

Andy Logan had given up his Sunday to stand in for Casualty Officer Bob Merrick, who was off on one of his wicked weekends. Andy was inclined to be grumpy when Laurel brought in a lad with a persistent nose-bleed.

'Don't keep trying to sniff it back, son, or you'll find yourself being sick,' he said with some impatience. 'Head forward, pinch the bridge like this, right? Nurse will get you some ice to hold there. If it doesn't stop we'll pack it, but I think you'll find it'll be all right in a while.'

Laurel took the boy out and handed him over to Rosemary with instructions on how to put crushed ice into a plastic bag to act as a haemostatic. She was about to take the next patient's card when the mother with the small girl who'd been bitten by her rabbit rushed up to Laurel in a great state of agitation.

'Oh, Nurse, I'm so glad you're here, because you know all about it. I had to bring 'er back this morning because we found the rabbit had died!' said the woman, her voice tragic.

Laurel cast her mind back. 'Oh, the one that bit her?' She turned a giggle into a cough behind her hand. 'Well, what . . . ?'

'I wondered about rabies 'n that,' the mother went on anxiously.

'I see. Well, I don't think you need to worry . . . but perhaps you'd like to have a word with the doctor.'

In the examination room she explained the situation to the long-suffering Andy. '. . . and she's worried because . . . the rabbit died!'

'Ah!' said Andy, taking the child's hand and inspecting the small cut, keeping an admirably solemn expression. 'I don't think rabbits can pass on anything very nasty. Poor rabbit, I should say, wouldn't you, Nurse?'

He exchanged a whimsical grin with Laurel, his customary sense of humour returning. 'Just put a clean dressing on it for her.'

With a fresh plaster applied to the finger, Laurel sent mother and child happily on their way.

As she was passing the office Sister Maguire beckoned to her. 'There's an RTA arriving . . . will you meet the ambulance?'

'Okay, Sister.' Laurel made for the entrance and within a few moments the ambulance drew up outside. She called for a porter to bring a trolley as the driver swung down.

He had a few words with her before opening up

the doors. 'Italian guy, drove into a lamppost. He's pretty cut about the face, but the main trouble is the steering-wheel caught him in the throat and chest. He's having a bit of bother breathing. The Alpha-Romeo was a write-off. He was lucky to get out in one piece.'

Laurel went to greet the victim as he was lifted out on a stretcher and transferred to the hospital trolley. He was a personable young man, olive-skinned and dark-eyed, with rich black curly hair.

'Hallo!' she said, in a compassionate voice, taking his hand and feeling for his pulse at the same time. 'You had an argument with a lamppost, I hear.' Her eyes took in the livid contusions around his neck as well as the abrasions to his face. He was sweating profusely and turned anguished eyes to hers, taking short panting breaths. 'All right, love,' she said gently, 'We'll try and make you more comfortable.'

They wheeled him quickly to an examination room, Laurel noting with concern his laboured efforts to breathe as the swelling in his bruised throat restricted his air passage. Rosemary, dogging her footsteps, hovered uncertainly. 'Help me get his clothes off and get me an examination gown,' Laurel prompted.

Very carefully they eased off the expensive suede jacket and hip-hugging trousers, trying to cause him as little stress as possible, propping him up to make his breathing easier. Laurel was alarmed by a certain blueness creeping beneath the olive skin. Covering him with a cellular blanket, she said, 'Stay with him, Rosemary, while I fetch a doctor.'

Outside she managed to grab Moira Carp making her regal way out of the doctors' office. 'Will you please come and take a look at this patient? He's badly bruised about the throat, possibly some fractured ribs as well. He doesn't look too good.'

The reception clerk had hurried after them to take details and now she handed the admission card to Dr Carp.

'Mr . . . Rinaldo?' said Moira, studying the card as she went in to see the patient. 'How are you feeling?'

'Bad!' he rasped, pointing to his throat.

'Yes, you've got some nasty bruising there,' Moira said, beginning her routine examination in a leisurely fashion.

Laurel frowned. She was becoming even more alarmed at the patient's colour. His face was purpling beneath the grazes, his fight for breath becoming even more frantic.

'Dr Carp,' she murmured in urgent undertones, 'shouldn't we get him along to Resus?'

'Mm?' said Moira, reaching into the pocket of her white coat for her stethoscope. 'Oh, I don't think that's necessary.' She seemed not to appreciate the imminent danger.

All at once Mr Rinaldo began to thrash about, making strangled stertorous noises, clutching at his throat.

'Quick! He's going to arrest!' hissed Laurel as the patient made a choking sound in a last unavailing effort to draw breath. Then he was still.

With all hands to the trolley, they raced towards the resuscitation room. A porter, well used to life and death dramas, lent his weight to speed their passage. Sister Maguire poked her head out of the office as they flew past. 'Get the crash team!' mouthed Laurel.

Reaching the resuscitation room, Moira Carp's poise deserted her. She literally wrung her hands, eyeing the inert patient. 'Oh God! We've lost him.'

'Emergency trachy!' Laurel darted to get out a tracheostomy pack.

Moira paled as Laurel tore off the covering and held it out to her. Her hands were shaking. Her desperate expression changed to one of immense relief as Bruce Tyson came striding into the room, followed by anaesthetist and houseman. Sizing up the situation, he grabbed the scalpel from the tray in Laurel's hands and made a rapid skilful incision into Mr Rinaldo's throat, just below the thyroid.

Laurel put the cuffed airway into his outstretched hand. He inserted it into the trachea. They waited . . . and everyone breathed sighs of relief as they heard the sweet sound of air being drawn into the patient's lungs.

'That was a near thing,' said Bruce Tyson, straightening up after closing the skin around the operation site, 'Quick thinking on someone's part.' He cast his eyes around the small group.

Moira gave him a honeyed smile. 'Yes, I would have done it if you hadn't arrived.'

Laurel's palms were sweating, but a wave of happiness washed over her at the knowledge that she had been equal to the crisis. She hadn't proved useless as in her nightmare. It didn't matter that Moira had taken the credit for herself.

'He'll have to go to ITU,' Bruce said over his shoulder to Laurel. 'Ring Sister and tell her to expect him will you? And put up a dextrose/saline drip,' he went on, turning to Moira. 'He's badly shocked. Better cross-match some blood while you're about it.'

Satisfied that he had done all that was required of him for the moment, the registrar left them to it. Panic over and the tracheostomy working well, the other details were attended to.

With a porter guiding one end of the trolley and Rosemary the other, Laurel accompanied Mr Rinaldo to the ward, holding his drip aloft. He had regained a hazy consciousness and laid a limp hand on her arm, unspoken gratitude in his dark eyes.

'You're going to be all right, love,' she murmured comfortingly.

'That Dr Carp!' said Rosemary indignantly, when they had left the patient in the care of ITU, 'If it had been up to her I bet he wouldn't have made it.'

The second shift had come on by the time they returned to the department. Rosemary went to lunch and Laurel went back to Resus to make sure that all was in order there before she went off for her half-day. It was nearly two o'clock before she was ready to leave.

Ahead of her, immaculate in a light grey suit, Bruce Tyson emerged from the doctors' office, also on his way out. Reaching the swing-doors, he paused to hold them open for her. 'Ah, the unflappable Nurse Swann,' he said, the gleam in his eyes belying his solemn expression. 'I'm glad to find you didn't crack under the strain today.'

They stood together on the forecourt. A light breeze ruffled Laurel's hair and she smoothed it back, returning levelly, 'and neither will Nurse Bates with a little more experience. It doesn't help if juniors get bawled out.'

His shrewd eyes looked her over, his lean face inscrutable. 'You've had no lunch yet?' he said abruptly.

'No, not yet.'

'Then you'd better have some with me. Come along.' Taking her elbow, he started to propel her in the direction of the car park.

She pulled back, her legs feeling oddly weak. 'B-but I'm not dressed for a lunch-date,' she faltered, contrasting her own workaday uniform coat with his smart clothes. 'I feel awfully grubby.'

'Well, I'll run you home first if you want to change,' he returned with some impatience.

'But I've got my own car here,' she pointed out, having to double her steps to keep pace with him as he continued to urge her along.

'My dear girl, will you stop procrastinating? I've never met such an argumentative creature.' Discounting her protests, he guided her to where his gleaming maroon Rover sat waiting. Unlocking the car, he climbed in and pushed open the passenger door for her. She slid into the comfortable fawn leather seat beside him, feeling dwarfed by his bulk.

'So you want to go home first?'

'Please, if you don't mind. It's only a ten minute drive.' She gave him directions as he manoeuvred the car out of the park and into the main stream of traffic.

In the silence that followed, Laurel racked her brains for an intelligent conversational opening. She was not usually at a loss for words but for once she was dumbstruck as she sat gripping her bag on her knees, stealing surreptitious glances at the husky man beside her. After what seemed like an eternity, they arrived outside the house without having exchanged another word.

'A-are you sure you don't mind waiting?' she ventured.

He checked the clock on his dashboard. 'Well, don't be all day. I'll give you five minutes. Scoot!' Leaning across her, he pushed open the car door. She caught the potent male scent of him as their bodies brushed. Her breath came quickly. Slipping out of the car, she ran for the shabby front door of the semi-detached house, feeling for the key in her raincoat pocket on the way.

'Where's the fire?' queried Emma, coming from the bathroom as Laurel rushed upstairs.

'Can't stop!' She sped on to her bedroom. 'Being taken to lunch . . . he's timing me!'

Emma stopped in her tracks and went to peep out of the front bedroom window. 'It's Tyson!' she exclaimed, rubbing sleepy blue eyes. 'Good Lord, what have you done to deserve that?'

Wriggling out of her uniform and pulling on her dark green sweater dress, Laurel dashed a comb through her hair. 'Think he intends to lecture me on the art of staying cool!' She kicked off her duty shoes and put on a pair of high heels. 'Tell you all about it later. Cheerio!' Grabbing her fawn jacket, she sped down the stairs and was gone, leaving Emma gazing after her, nonplussed.

'How's that?' panted Laurel, her cheeks pink with hurrying, her eyes shining as he opened the car door at her approach.

He checked the clock. 'Not bad.'

'I didn't win the hundred yards for nothing!' she quipped as they drove away.

His mouth twisted into a patronising smile. 'Not an athlete too? Is there no end to your accomplishments?'

She hadn't intended to boast. 'It was only a joke,' she explained, blushing.

'Sometimes I'm slow to catch on, they tell me.'

She flung him a suspicious glance. Was he laughing at her? It was hard to tell from that enigmatic face. All the same, it was a fascinating face; a mixture of strength, gentleness and hauteur. But not a person to be trifled with, she thought, and wondered how he had come by that small scar which broke the perfect line of his attractive mouth.

The morning mist had cleared and the sun shone invitingly as he drove across Blackheath's green spaces in the direction of Greenwich. Parking the car on a roughly gravelled site near the Seamen's Hospital, he walked her the short distance to the Trafalgar Inn.

He ushered her into the cocktail bar. 'We're rather late for lunch, but I expect they can find us something.'

A waiter approached them with a polite bow,

menus in hand. 'Good afternoon, Mr Tyson.' Obviously he was a regular there, Laurel decided as she studied the bill of fare.

When they had ordered she tried again to think of something to say, anything to break the disconcerting effect those bold blue eyes had upon her.

'How did you come to be at the Heathside when . . . on Presentation Day?' she asked, sipping her pre-lunch sherry, and making an effort to keep her hand steady.

'My sister-in-law also trained there. Perhaps you knew her . . . Jean Miles?'

'Oh! Oh yes, but only vaguely. It's a big place, and she wasn't in my set.' His sister-in-law? So he was married, her subconscious recorded. But he must be well into his thirties, and it wasn't really surprising for a man of his charisma.

It did help her to relax a little, knowing that the lunch invitation was nothing more than a social gesture. Perhaps it was his way of making amends for being such a boor the previous day, since he was hardly the sort of man to apologise. She began to feel more kindly disposed towards him. The drink also helped her to unwind and by the time they were shown to a table overlooking the river in the now fairly empty restaurant, Laurel was more like her usual confident self.

'I'd never actually been in on an emergency tracheostomy,' she confessed, tackling her steak with relish. 'It's a bit savage, isn't it?'

'But very effective. The only possible course in Rinaldo's case.'

'He'll be all right, will he? He seemed a nice guy.'

Bruce Tyson forked a mushroom into his mouth. 'No reason why he shouldn't be, once the swelling goes down.'

'It was quite hectic this morning, for a Sunday,' she went on. 'I'm off now, and all day tomorrow, thank goodness.' She raised bright eyes and met his, observing her closely.

'And what will you do with your day off?' he enquired, 'Go home?'

'No.' She paused. 'I don't go home too much these days.'

She had spoken without thinking and he was quick to pick her up on the remark. 'Any particular reason for that?'

Laurel shrugged and sipped her wine. 'My father and I are . . . well, we're not the best of pals at the moment.'

'Oh, so it's not only registrars you fall out with?'

She was not going to be provoked. 'I haven't fallen out with him. Things have become a little strained, that's all.' Without meaning to she found herself telling him about her father and Ingrid. 'Dad's a GP and she's matron of a private clinic he's concerned with. She's only twelve years older than me. I know I shouldn't mind,' said Laurel with a rueful smile, 'but I can't help it. I hate the thought of anyone taking my mother's place.'

He made no comment as he finished his own drink. 'Where is your home?' he asked presently.

'Just the other side of Sevenoaks.'

Bruce Tyson glanced at her with sudden interest. 'Would your father be Alexander Brendan-Swann?'

'Yes. Do you know him?' asked Laurel in surprise.

'I know the name. I saw it on a letter when he referred one of his patients to us.'

She remembered. 'Oh yes, he did mention that he'd sent somebody the last time we spoke on the phone.'

The waiter came to clear their plates. 'Would you like a sweet?'

'No, thank you. Just coffee,' she said.

The registrar checked his wristwatch. 'None for me . . . and I'll have the bill please.'

'Are you pushed for time?' she asked.

'I do have to get back.'

She wished she had not asked for the coffee. She swallowed it quickly when it came.

Making her way to the foyer while he settled up, she waited for him to follow. He pushed through the street door, holding it open for her. As she stepped out one of her heels caught in the brass-covered doorsill. She would have pitched headlong had his arms not closed around her.

Her heart beat wildly at their close bodily contact. 'History repeats itself,' he observed drily, his breath warm on her cheek.

She struggled to free herself from his constraining arms. 'For heaven's sake, you can let me go now, I'm all right,' she gasped, feeling decidedly shaky.

When he did release her she almost lost her balance again. One leg seemed curiously shorter than the other. Picking up her foot to investigate, she muttered, 'Oh, blast!'

He stooped to retrieve the heel she had lost, handing it to her with exasperating cheerfulness. 'I'm surprised you don't break your neck regularly on these stilts. Can you make it to the car . . . or do you want me to carry you?'

'Don't be ridiculous. Of course I can make it.' She hobbled along beside him for a few yards with as much dignity as she could muster, peg-leg fashion. Then she gave up the struggle, took off both shoes and padded along barefoot.

'Ruinous to tights, I should have thought,' he murmured with ill-concealed amusement.

At last they reached the car park, but attempting to hobble across the sharp flints was torture, like walking on a bed of nails, and she winced visibly. With an expression of impatience he swept her off her feet and with perfect ease carried her like a child, setting her down beside the car.

'Thank you,' she said meekly.

He unlocked the door for her to get in. 'I'll take you back to the hospital to pick up your own car. I suppose you will be able to drive it like that?'

'I keep a pair of flatties in the car.'

'So common sense does triumph over vanity when necessary?'

Sarcastic swine, she thought, scowling and gritting her teeth at his superior expression. She felt thoroughly humiliated and near to tears. What an idiot he must think her. Not that she cared what he thought, she told herself crossly. Outside of work she was unlikely to have anything more to do with him.

'It must be tough on your wife when you work

weekends,' she ventured in an effort to take the spotlight off herself.

'My wife?' His face was stony. 'I don't have a wife now.'

Laurel shrank with dismay. Hell! She had done it again. 'Oh, I—I'm sorry . . . I—I just presumed . . . when you spoke about your sister-in-law . . .'

'Then you shouldn't presume. Presumptions are always dangerous.'

You obnoxious brute, she thought, throwing him a black look and fighting back the urge to explode. If he was divorced, then he probably deserved it. He must have been impossible to live with.

Their journey back was completed in silence. 'Thank you for the lunch,' she said primly, when they arrived back at the hospital.

Opening the car door, she clutched her shoes and ran across the tarmac to the refuge of her own Mini, where she sat for a few moments trying to simmer down. Then she fished for her old shoes under the driving seat and slowly eased her way through the parked cars. She threw a baleful glare in the direction of his Rover as she passed. But it was a wasted effort. Bruce had disappeared.

CHAPTER THREE

IT WAS almost five o'clock before Laurel arrived back at the house. Glad to find Emma at home, she relieved her ruffled feelings with a graphic account of her impromptu lunch with Bruce Tyson and the subsequent disastrous happenings. 'So that's the second time he's stopped me hitting the deck, but he's such an arrogant beast, I could crown him!'

Emma, rinsing some tights at the kitchen sink, gave her a wan smile as she turned to hang her washing on the airer.

'I mean, I thought he was trying to make up for being a stinker yesterday, but no . . .' Laurel broke off in mid-sentence, realising that Emma was only half-listening. 'Are you all right, Em?'

Her friend's eyes brimmed with sudden tears. She gave a watery laugh. 'Oh, don't take any notice of me. I'm a bit down, that's all. I phoned Phil to remind him I was off nights and that I'd be able to see him this evening, but he wasn't there. Gone away for the weekend . . . a houseboat party on the Thames, someone told me. I just think he might've said.'

'Oh!' Laurel didn't quite know what else to say. The truth was she was not over-impressed with Emma's boyfriend; he was a houseman she had met at her training hospital. Although she had only a brief acquaintance with him, Laurel suspected he was a shallow character. He was forever letting Emma down. And he had a roving eye. Dilys said he had even made a pass at her once.

'Well, maybe he forgot about you coming off nights, and maybe this was too good a scene to pass up. I mean, housemen don't get too much fun, do they? They work pretty hard.'

Emma blew her nose and shook back her heavy fair hair. 'I know all that, but . . . well . . . I'm almost certain he's seeing someone else.'

'Oh!' said Laurel again. 'Well, Em, if he is two-timing you, I should tell him to get lost. You'll get over it. I know I felt depressed when Gary ditched me, but then I decided no guy was going to louse up my life.'

'But I don't think you loved him that much, did you? I mean, *really* loved him. I know you were fond of him.' She sniffed. 'Somehow I don't care who Phil plays around with so long as he comes back to me.'

Laurel sighed and kept her thoughts to herself. 'Cheer up, Em,' she said. 'I expect he'll be all repentant when he knows he's missed out on seeing you. Look, why don't we go to the flicks? There's a replay of Walt Disney's Jungle Book on at the local. I'd like to see that again, wouldn't you?'

'Okay,' agreed Emma, 'I'll go and put my face on.'

Laurel followed her upstairs to find some other shoes. 'I'll need to drop my car in at the garage on the way,' she called. 'Some blighter must have reversed into me in the car park—my rear light's shattered. We can pick it up on the way home. It shouldn't take them long.'

The film put them both in better spirits, but calling in at the garage to collect the car, Laurel found it had not yet been fixed.

'Sorry, love,' the proprietor said, 'my mechanic had to go off early, and I've been kept busy on the pumps myself. By the way, I wouldn't advise you to drive much further on those tyres, a couple of them are bald. Shall we fit you some new ones?'

'Oh, blow!' Laurel screwed up her nose. 'Can't afford new tyres this month. Better just do the light for now. I only make short trips. I'll have to be careful.'

The garage man looked dubious. 'Better watch out or you could fall foul of the law,' he warned.

'Well, okay, perhaps I won't use it till I get them done. It'll have to wait till next pay-day, though.'

They caught the bus home, but for Laurel the news had dampened the cheering effect of the film. She pondered whether she could really afford to run a car, even though her father did pay for things like insurance. She didn't want to go to him for new tyres.

Over the next few days she had only brief glimpses of Bruce Tyson in the course of her work. She had wondered what his attitude towards her would be after their lunch together, but when they did meet he seemed barely to acknowledge her existence. She might have been a stranger. His indifference peeved her.

Moira Carp, on the other hand, appeared to be

on very intimate terms with the registrar. They were often to be found together and she flirted with him outrageously. Laurel decided that Dr Carp was not her most favourite person, although it was no concern of hers that the girl was blatantly chasing Bruce. They were both grown adults, entitled to do as they pleased. If that was the kind of woman he liked, well good luck to him.

It was the following Saturday that fate flung her into the registrar's company again, when the crash team was called to a cardiac arrest. All were feeling gratified at the successful outcome of their efforts, and Laurel took the patient off to ITU glad to have played her part in his recovery.

She returned to the department, reporting to the office to go off duty at four-thirty. Both Andy Logan and Bruce Tyson were sitting there with Sister Maguire, who was speaking on the telephone. 'Oh, here she is now,' said Sister, beckoning to Laurel, 'I'll hand you over.' She passed over the receiver, explaining, 'It's about your father . . . he's not too well.'

A premonition of disaster made Laurel's stomach turn over. 'Hallo?' she said.

The voice that came over the wire was Ingrid's. 'I thought I ought to let you know, Laurel, although your father did say I wasn't to alarm you. He's had a severe gastric bleed. He's at the clinic with me now and Dr Grantham has seen him and we're giving him a transfusion. I think he really would love to see you, though.'

Laurel paled, her legs threatening not to support her. She propped herself against the desk, hardly aware of the interested eyes upon her. 'Oh dear! How is he . . . is he . . . ?'

'Well, he's looking much better for the transfusion. Luckily I was with him when he collapsed, so I was able to get Dr Grantham straight away. When could you come?'

'I'm off now . . . I'll come at once.' She suddenly remembered the bald tyres. 'Oh! My car's not serviceable at the moment . . . and there's a wretched rail strike. I'll have to see if there's a Green Line. Anyway, thanks for telling me, Ingrid. Give Dad my love, and I'll be with you as soon as I can.'

Andy Logan looked from her to the registrar. 'You're going to Tonbridge tonight, aren't you, Bruce? Couldn't you give her a lift?'

'I could,' he answered. 'It wouldn't be out of my way.'

Moira Carp had come in at the tail end of the conversation. 'And who is claiming your services in such a hurry?' she drawled, looking archly at Bruce.

The situation was explained to her. 'Oh well, in that case I suppose I shall have to let you have him, Nurse,' she conceded.

With a tight-lipped smile, Bruce rose from his chair. 'I'm almost ready to go. Shall I pick you up at the house in, say, half an hour?'

'Thank you very much,' said Laurel.

'And I'll let the Nursing Officer know, dear,' Sister Maguire said. 'Take as much time as you need . . . I hope you'll find he's not too bad.'

Back at the house Laurel discarded her uniform

for a pleated skirt, heather-coloured jumper and her fawn jacket. She threw a few things into her overnight bag and was ready and waiting when Bruce called for her.

Seated in the car alongside him, she had to bite her lips to keep control. To other people in trouble she brought peace of mind with her calming efficiency. It was a very different matter, she found, when you were personally involved.

They sped along in silence for a while, Bruce concentrating on traffic hazards, strong hands lightly steering the wheel. Pulling up at traffic lights, he cast her a sideways glance. 'You must try not to worry. I'm sure your father is being well looked after.' His quietly confident tone was reassuring.

'I—I feel terrible,' she confessed, chewing her thumbnail, 'because I've been off-hand with him lately. I haven't been much of a comfort to him since my mother died.'

'He probably understands better than you think. Bereavement affects people in many different ways. And we all have feelings of regret about the might-have-been. No need to feel guilty. His collapse had nothing to do with you.'

Now they had left the suburbs behind and were into the lush Kent countryside. It was warm for late April. Bruce had the window down and his jacket off, so she was very conscious of his vital, muscled body beneath the fine striped-cotton shirt.

In the gathering dusk orchards gleamed pink and white with apple blossom. For ever afterwards the faint perfume, wafting in on the breeze, would remind her of this journey and the dominant presence of the man beside her. She couldn't help being aware of his physical attractions, despite her personal worries. Stealing a glance at his lean profile and the determined set of his chin, she felt a sense of security in being with him, authoritarian though he was.

'I'm sorry if I spoiled your weekend plans,' she said at length.

'Plans? What plans?' There was a suggestion of the mind-blowing smile that occasionally softened his stern features.

'I—I was thinking of what Dr Carp said . . .'

'Moira? Oh, we had no definite plans.'

Laurel felt absurdly pleased. 'She's quite something, isn't she? Beauty and brains.'

'She's not unique in that. It depends what type you go for.' There was a touch of amused condescension in his deep voice and she shrank into her shell again. It was unnerving the effect he had upon her. She found him both fascinating and infuriating. And he was probably well aware of his own charms. She made a conscious effort to direct her thoughts back to more important matters than the war of the sexes.

Traffic was light that evening. They made good speed towards her destination. After driving through Sevenoaks, Laurel pointed out the long private road which led through heavily wooded grounds to the clinic.

It was housed in a large old country mansion. Creeper climbed over the rose-brick walls and tall, ornate chimneys, now no longer in use, bore witness to a bygone age.

Bruce brought the car to a halt outside the solid oak, iron-studded front door. 'Where will you stay tonight?' he asked, in the manner of a concerned parent.

'At home, I expect. It's not far from here.'

'You can get a taxi, I suppose?'

'Oh, yes.'

He eased his bulk out of the car and took her weekend case from the back seat. 'Here you are, then. I hope you'll find things better than you imagine.' Hands in pockets, he stood watching while she pulled the bell in the large porchway, waiting for the door to open. Then, giving her a casual wave, he returned to the car and drove off.

The picturesque old family seat had been modernised inside for its present use but still retained its air of aristocratic opulence. There were some twenty private rooms and a number of two-bedded ones. The small but up-to-date theatre and X-ray room could cope with all but the most complicated of cases.

Laurel was admitted by the receptionist into a gracious blue-carpeted hall. 'I'll phone Matron and tell her you're here,' she said.

Ingrid was with her in a few minutes. She had the blue-eyed good looks of her Swedish nationality, neatly coiled blonde hair and perfect white teeth when she smiled. Laurel could quite understand why her father found the girl so appealing.

'You have been quick,' Ingrid said, extending both hands in welcome. 'Alex will be so glad to see you.'

'How is he?' Laurel asked anxiously.

'Well, he lost quite a lot of blood . . . he was in shock at first, very dehydrated, but he's looking much better now. Dr Grantham will be doing a gastroscopy in the morning to see what exactly is going on in the stomach. We've settled him down for the night now. He's probably sleeping, but come and see.'

Laurel followed her up the curving stairway to the first floor, then along a wide gallery into a single room. Dr Swann lay propped up in bed, eyes closed. The uniformed nurse checking the flow of blood dripping steadily into his arm, smiled and left as they came in.

Watching her father's quiet breathing, Laurel saw the pallor underlying his normally ruddy cheeks. His hands lay limp, loose-skinned on the counterpane. 'W—we'd better not disturb him,' she whispered, fighting against tears.

Ingrid led her gently from the room. 'You would like to stay? You can spend the night in my flat,' she suggested, 'then you can see him first thing in the morning, before he goes to theatre.'

Laurel nodded. 'Thank you, that would be lovely.'

In her private apartment Ingrid showed her guest to a chintz-covered armchair in the cosy sitting-room. She poured sherry for them both and sat down opposite her. 'I wondered how you would get here without your car. We are not easy to get to by public transport.'

'A friend from the hospital happened to be coming this way—he brought me.'

'A special friend?' Ingrid's eyes were curious.

'No, not special.'

They talked quietly about her father and his collapse. After some hesitation Ingrid ventured: 'You know . . . we had decided to get married in June, but we may have to put it off for a while now. Your father was a little concerned as to how you would feel about it.' With a pucker between her brows she went on, 'I am not wishing to take your mother's place, Laurel. I know I could never do that. But you would not wish your father to spend the rest of his days alone? I want only to make him happy. We have much in common.'

It flashed upon Laurel that she had no right whatever to object to her father remarrying. He had been a loving husband when her mother was alive; he deserved some companionship in his remaining years. And after all, she had more or less abandoned him for her career.

Remorse washed over her. 'Ingrid, I'm sorry if I've seemed . . . well, if you've felt any hostility. I didn't mean it. Mother and I were very close. But if you can make Dad happy, then I shall be grateful.'

'I do love him,' Ingrid said simply, her eyes over-bright as they looked at each other.

Impulsively Laurel jumped up to kiss her and they clung together for a few moments, both a little embarrassed at their show of emotion.

Ingrid cleared her throat. 'I expect you are hungry,' she said briskly. 'I shall find us some supper, and then you can sleep in my spare room. Come . . . I show you where it is.'

She took Laurel along a passageway to a small but pleasant room. There were turquoise damask curtains at its mullioned windows and rugs on polished boards. The bed was a modern divan with a turquoise coverlet and a matching wash-basin gleamed in one corner. 'Perhaps you'd like to freshen up,' Ingrid said, 'then come back to my room and we'll eat.'

Early next morning Laurel was able to see her father. He greeted her in pleased surprise. 'Darling! So naughty Ingrid did send for you. I told her not to. But it's good to see you all the same.' He took her hand and smiled feebly. 'Lot of fuss about nothing this is.'

'No it isn't, and you know it,' she chided.

'Oh well, I suppose it does no harm to be on the receiving end once in a while. Makes you see things from the patient's point of view, eh? God, I'm dry! Nothing to drink since last night.'

She gazed at him lovingly. 'Not much longer and you'll be able to drink all you want.' Having him to herself she attempted to bridge the slight gulf that had grown between them. 'Daddy, I—I had a long talk with Ingrid last night. She tells me you're planning to get married as soon as you're well enough.' The words tumbled out and he looked at her warily.

'Yes, we are. That's if she doesn't mind getting landed with an old crock like me. What d'you think about it, eh?'

There was a lump in Laurel's throat as she looked at the anxious face beneath the thick, silvering hair. He really was a handsome old darling. 'You're not a crock . . . and I think she's a lovely lady. You're very lucky to have found her.'

His eyes crinkled at the corners. She could tell he was pleased, even though he just grunted, patted his tummy and said, 'Let's hope they don't find any nasties in here.'

'Well now, just you behave yourself and do what you're told.' Laurel grinned. 'Doctors are the very worst patients. Glad I'm not nursing you. I shall stick around and see you again when you've had your gastroscopy.'

It was not a lengthy procedure. With injections of Valium as a throat relaxant, Atropine to dry secretions and Fortral as a sedative, Dr Swann was back in his room in under an hour, still sleepy. He would have had no awareness of the plastic tube with its magnifying lens that had been passed into his stomach so that the damage could be diagnosed.

There was great relief all round that no signs of cancer had been found, which was probably what Dr Swann had been fearing. The cause of the bleed was identified as a duodenal ulcer.

'And now that we have Cimetidine, there's every hope that the ulcer will heal up nicely without recourse to surgery,' Dr Grantham told Laurel cheerfully, speaking with her in Ingrid's office. 'He should be up and about again in two or three weeks.'

Richard Grantham appeared to have something else on his mind. He put a fatherly arm around Laurel's slim shoulders. 'My dear, I haven't had a chance to tell you how sorry I am that you and Gary have decided . . .'

'Oh, don't worry about that, Uncle Richard,' she cut in with a light laugh. 'I'm not heartbroken. I suppose we more or less drifted into a relationship, and we drifted out again.'

He looked regretful as he gave her a squeeze. 'All the same, I should have liked you for a daughter-in-law. Now some other lucky chap will take you from us.'

She gave him a swift, affectionate kiss on the cheek. 'You always were a smooth talker,' she said.

The telephone rang and Ingrid answered it. 'For you, Laurel.' She passed over the receiver.

It was a surprise to hear the voice of Bruce Tyson on the other end of the line. 'Good morning, Laurel. And how is your father?'

'Oh, he's fine, thank you. It was a duodenal ulcer, but they hope it won't be necessary to operate.'

'Splendid. When are you going back?'

'Well, possibly tonight. He's quite cheerful and feeling stronger since his transfusion.' She looked across at Ingrid and smiled. 'He gets VIP treatment here, so I don't have to worry.'

'Good!' Bruce said. 'I shall be coming back around eight tonight. I'll pick you up, if that would help?'

She hesitated. 'I don't like to trouble you . . .'

'No trouble,' he said.

Later that day there was an almost festive atmosphere around Dr Swann's bed. Plans for the wedding were openly discussed now that Laurel had cleared the air.

'And who's this fellow I hear about, dancing

attendance on you?' her father wanted to know.

'He's our surgical registrar, and he isn't dancing attendance on me. He happened to have business in Tonbridge.'

'What's wrong with your own car?'

'I need two new tyres. Couldn't afford it this month.'

'Get it done, girl. Send the bill to me.'

'Oh, Dad,' she protested, 'I'm trying to be independent.'

'For heaven's sake! Can't a chap do something for his only daughter?'

She laughed. 'Well, thank you. Shall I send you a bill for your wedding present as well?'

He took a playful swipe at her. 'Cheeky puss.'

The drive back to London that evening was a much less tense affair than the drive down. Having made her peace with Ingrid and her father, Laurel felt positively lighthearted. She chatted away happily to Bruce, telling him about the clinic, and her father's practice, and the proposed wedding.

'So you changed your mind about the age difference?' he taunted, with an air of mild indulgence. 'You don't think it matters?'

'Well, age is a relative thing, isn't it? I mean, some people are born old and others are young at heart for ever. My father is one of those.'

'What a wise head there is on those young shoulders.' There was a satirical twist to his mouth. 'But I'm glad to find you in better spirits. By the way, our Italian friend, Paolo Rinaldo, was asking after you the other day.'

'Your emergency trachy? I'm surprised he even

remembered me, the state he was in. How is he?'

'Much better and breathing more easily now that the swelling has subsided. He had a few bruised ribs and a cracked sternum, but he should be discharged in a day or so.' After a pause Bruce went on, 'It appears he thought he had died and that you must be an angel when you were taking him up to the ward.'

Laurel giggled. 'Some angel. He *must* have been hallucinating.'

'Oh, your halo is pretty bright in that quarter,' remarked Bruce with a wry smile. 'Apparently he attributes his deliverance to you.'

'But it was you who did the necessary.'

He cast a teasing glance in her direction. 'I don't happen to have a cute little nose and eyes like emeralds . . . his words, not mine,' he added.

She felt herself blushing and hurried to change the subject. 'Did you have a good time in Tonbridge?'

'Yes, I always enjoy my visits there.' It left her none the wiser as to the purpose of his visit.

It was nine-thirty when they drew up outside her home. She felt obligated to ask him in for a coffee at least.

Leaning back against his seat, he treated her to a long provocative stare. 'Is that all I'm offered for my services?'

She caught her breath in confusion, not knowing quite what he meant. 'We-ell, I could run to a toasted cheese sandwich as well, if you're hungry?'

There was a hint of devilment in the deep blue eyes which continued to regard her steadily. She flushed and fidgeted, and the handbag on her lap slipped down by the gear lever. They both bent to pick it up, banging their heads together.

'Sorry,' she said as they came up and their cheeks brushed. He turned towards her. For one heart-stopping moment she thought he was going to kiss her. Then his expression changed, his hand brushed past her to push open the door. 'Be off with you,' he said, gruffly, 'I'm on my way to have a drink with Moira.'

Waiting only long enough for him to pass her weekend case from the back seat, she hurried from the car and ran towards the house. On the doorstep she took a long breath before letting herself in. Damn the man! What an odious, self-opinionated, ego-maniac he was. She couldn't think of enough disparaging words to describe him.

There was a light in the living-room and sounds of music. Laurel looked in and found Emma sprawled on the sofa, munching a Mars bar as she watched TV.

'Hi!' she greeted Laurel. 'How's your dad?'

'Oh, he's going to be okay.' Flinging off her jacket and relaxing in an armchair, Laurel swallowed her vexation and tried to appear bright.

'It was a duodenal ulcer,' she went on to explain, 'but they're treating it with drugs. Barring complications he should be on his feet again soon.'

Emma smiled. 'Oh, good. I thought you looked a bit upset when you came in, so I wondered if things were bad.'

'Not with Dad.' Laurel ground her teeth. 'I've just had it up to here with Bruce Tyson.'

'I heard he'd given you a lift,' Emma said, 'I thought it was rather decent of him.'

Laurel grunted. 'Huh! It wasn't his idea. Andy Logan more or less press-ganged him into it.'

'Well, he's not the kind of bloke to be press-ganged into anything he didn't want to do. Lots of people would have been glad to be in your shoes . . . a long and intimate drive with the beautiful Brucey!'

'They're welcome to my share . . . but what are you doing here on your own? I thought Phil was due to come down this weekend?'

Emma breathed a long sigh. 'He rang to say he was too tired because he'd been up half the night. So to save him the journey I thought I'd go up there and surprise him. Too tired! When I got there he was entertaining this bird in his room. I walked straight out again.'

'Good for you. What happens now?'

'We had a showdown on the phone when I got back. I told him I was through with being messed about and that he'd better choose between her and me.'

Emma's soft blue eyes clouded over and her lips trembled. 'H-he said, okay, let's call it a day.' She shrugged helplessly. 'So I suppose it's finished.'

'Men!' Laurel seethed. 'You're better off without him you know, Em. You'd never have a moment's peace of mind if you married him.'

'I—I know . . . the trouble is, I still love him.' She brushed a hand across her eyes and sniffed.

They heard the sound of a key in the front door, followed by Dilys' laughter and male voices.

'Oh Lord,' muttered Emma, 'who's she brought back with her? Do I look a sight?'

'Go and blow your nose. I'll say you've got a cold.'

Emma dashed past Dilys as she came in with Andy Logan and Mike Spring, a fellow physiotherapist.

'What's up with her?' Dilys murmured to Laurel.

'She's got a cold coming on . . . nose dripping like a tap. Do you all want coffee? I'll go and make some.'

Dilys went over to switch off the television and put on the stereo. 'Make yourselves at home, boys. I'll go and help Laurel and then we can continue living it up. Got to unwind . . . not ready for bed yet.'

Outside in the kitchen she tackled Laurel. 'Is it that beast Phil again?'

Laurel nodded. 'They've split, permanently this time, I think. But pretend not to notice anything. We'll have to buck her up somehow.'

They carried the drinks through to the living-room as Emma came back, looking a little more composed.

'Hallo!' she said with a determined effort at gaiety, 'Good party, was it?'

'It would have been better if you'd been there,' piped up Mike Spring to Laurel's surprise. He was a somewhat shy and unassuming individual, not over-confident where the opposite sex was concerned.

'Well, now's your chance to dance with her,' put in Dilys. 'Come on, Andy.' She pulled him to his feet and they both began gyrating with abandon.

'Shall we?' Mike spoke to Emma with a hesitant smile, as though half expecting a refusal.

'I'll try not to give you my germs,' she said, going into his arms.

From the expression on Mike's face it was obvious to Laurel that even sharing a cold with Emma would be his idea of heaven.

Tapping her foot to the music, she sighed as she watched her friends. Unbidden, her thoughts returned to Bruce. She tried to picture herself with him in this informal kind of atmosphere. But she couldn't imagine him otherwise than urbanely professional or scathingly supercilious. There were times on the journey home when she had been lulled into thinking that he liked her a little; until that cat-and-mouse charade outside in the car. She guessed he knew very well that she thought he had been about to kiss her. Instead of which he had merely been amusing himself at her expense. And the crowning insult was his mention of Moira.

The sophisticated Moira Carp was probably his type anyway, she concluded, and it was immaterial to her. In any case, it was nothing short of lunacy to waste time thinking about a man who apparently believed you were beneath his notice.

The more she watched the others enjoying themselves the more depressed she felt. Presently she made her excuses and went up to bed.

CHAPTER FOUR

ON MONDAY morning the A and E department of the Riversdale Hospital seemed to be overrun with children. Scarcely had the staff finished their early morning cleaning and restocking of treatment rooms before the casualties began to arrive.

Sister Maguire popped her head into the coffee room where Laurel, Kathie Moran, Molly O'Brien and Rosemary were having their morning break. 'Query appendix abscess on its way,' she said. 'Will you go, Laurel?'

'Right, Sister.' Laurel finished her drink and went along to the ambulance entrance to await the arrival of the patient.

'Got a ten-year-old here for you, love,' said the ambulance driver coming round to open up the doors. 'Seems pretty poorly . . . his mum's with him.'

They transferred the feverish child to a hospital trolley. Laurel smiled at the anxious-faced mother and spoke kindly to the boy. 'Hallo! And what's your name?'

'Robin,' he answered, valiantly trying to keep a stiff upper lip.

She squeezed his hand comfortingly. 'Okay, Robin, let's see what we can do for you.'

The mother handed over a letter from their GP as they wheeled the boy to an examination bay.

'He's been sick all night,' she explained. 'He's kept nothing down since breakfast yesterday.'

'I see.' Laurel noted the flushed face and worried expression of the young patient. 'We'll just get you ready and then I'll bring the doctor.'

She exchanged the child's pyjamas for an examination gown, recorded his TPR and obtained a urine specimen before going in search of a casualty officer. Finding Andy Logan in the doctors' office, she gave him the letter from the GP. 'He's very nauseous,' she reported. 'Pains around the epigastric region. Nice little chap though, quite co-operative.'

Andy went along with her to make his routine examination. 'Just tell me when it hurts, son.' Gently he palpated the rigid abdomen, extracting a howl from the child as he pressed the right iliac fossa.

'Mmm . . . that seems conclusive enough.' He turned to the mother. 'He'll almost certainly need an operation, but I'll get someone else to take a look at him.' He went off to bleep Bruce Tyson, returning to say that the registrar would be down when he'd finished his rounds with the consultant.

'I hope we won't have to keep you waiting too long,' Laurel told the mother, with an apologetic smile. Leaving a vomit bowl handy, she went back to the office.

Her next charge was a six-year-old girl named Deirdre who had fallen over on her way to school, cutting her knee on a piece of glass. It was a deep cut. Laurel was pretty sure it would need a couple of stitches. She put the details in the doctors' office and presently Moira Carp came along to examine the wound.

Moira's charm was invariably reserved for the male population. She took scarcely any notice of the mother. 'Yes, it'll need a couple of sutures,' she said off-handedly. 'I'll be along in a minute.'

The child grew more and more apprehensive as she was taken along to theatre. She burst into stormy tears when Laurel popped her on the bed before opening up a suture pack in readiness. 'It's all right, love. It'll be over before you know it,' she comforted.

When Moira arrived and gloved up, the patient began to scream and kick even before she was touched.

'Oh, do be a good girl, Deirdre,' pleaded her embarrassed mother. 'I'll give you an extra fifty pence pocket money if you'll let the doctor do it.'

The promise had little effect on the squirming, frightened child. Moira lost her patience. 'Well, I can't waste any more time here,' she snapped. 'You'll have to wait until she comes to her senses.'

Laurel decided it was time for a little firmness. She took a controlling hold of Deirdre and said reassuringly, 'Just keep still dear, and it won't take a minute.' With the accompaniment of a couple of squeals the two stitches were inserted. 'There, that wasn't too bad, was it?' With a Kleenex Laurel mopped the tears from the resentful little face.

'Come back in five days to have the stitches out,' Moira instructed the mother.

Aside to the doctor, Laurel murmured, 'It's over a joint.'

'What? Oh, yes. Better make that ten days.'

'Don't forget you owe me fifty pee,' whined the child to her mother as they left.

Moira stripped off her gloves, her lip curling in distaste. 'Little horror! What she needed was a good smacked bottom, not extra pocket money.'

'Oh, the poor kid was just scared, I expect,' Laurel said sympathetically.

About to return to check on her previous patient, she caught sight of Andy with Bruce Tyson emerging from the doctors' office. Her stomach flipped at the sight of the registrar. Her immediate impulse was to turn and run, but she had to face him. 'Have you come to see young Robin?' she said in a matter-of-fact manner. 'This way.'

Bruce barely deigned to acknowledge her, but he greeted the mother with a courteous 'Good morning', and going over to the child, his smile was warm. 'Hallo, old son. Not feeling too good?'

Robin shook his head, his lips quivering.

As Andy gave a brief résumé of his findings, Bruce felt for the child's pulse and nodded in agreement. 'Right,' he said, 'I won't pull you about any more. We'll find you a bed in our children's ward and then have a look at what's going on in your tummy. Don't worry, old chap, you'll be asleep long before we do that. You won't know anything about it. You'll wake up in bed when it's all over. Okay?'

He lightly ruffled the boy's hair and Robin gave a wan smile. Taking the mother aside, Bruce had a quiet word with her before he left, setting her mind at ease and explaining that he would need her signature on the consent form for permission to operate.

In spite of her personal feelings of antagonism towards the man, Laurel could not help contrasting Bruce's handling of their young patient with Moira's unfeeling approach. He had a good way with children. What an enigma he was, she thought, at times so taciturn and overbearing and yet so compassionate and kindly when need be.

Calling a porter, she handed the case notes to Rosemary and asked her to accompany Robin and his mother up to the ward.

Back in the reception area, she was about to attend to the next patient when a young couple burst through the swing-doors and came rushing towards her. The woman clutched a baby in her arms. 'I—I went to pick her up for her feed . . . and she was like this!' Her eyes were stark with desperation. 'You can do something, can't you? Oh, please do something!'

Laurel took the baby and looked at it. It was blue in the face, not breathing. 'Wait in there,' she said, indicating the relatives' room, before rushing the infant straight through to Resus. She spoke into the intercom. 'Sister and doctor to Resus One, quickly please!'

It was fairly obvious to her that the baby was beyond help. Nevertheless she was already trying heart massage when Sister Maguire and Andy came post-haste in answer to her urgent call. 'Looks like a cot death,' she said.

Sister Maguire went to the phone and bleeped for the paediatrician. Andy took over the heart massage in the faint hope of a miracle. Dr Chris Goodman appeared with all speed and administered a shot of Adrenalin. They continued with the heart massage for a while, but all realised it was hopeless.

'Nice baby, too,' sighed Dr Goodman, making a careful examination of the infant. 'No signs of non-accidental injury. Looks perfectly well-nourished and cared for. Wish there was something we could have done.' He sighed again. 'You'd better inform the police and I'll get in touch with the GP. The parents will need his support. I'll have a word with them . . . where are they?'

'In the relatives' room,' said Laurel. She went with Dr Goodman to find the young couple.

'I'm so sorry . . . we did all we could,' explained the paediatrician gently.

The mother buried her face in her husband's chest and broke into violent sobs. 'Would you like to see her for a moment?' said Dr Goodman when her grief had subsided a little.

She nodded and Laurel led them back to the resuscitation room where Sister Maguire had wrapped the infant in a shawl. The woman clutched it to her, weeping afresh.

After a while they took the baby from her and led the parents away to a quiet place. Sister stayed with them, explaining that they were not to be worried about the police having to be informed. 'It's standard practice, my dears. We could all see that your baby has been well cared for. You mustn't blame yourselves. We only wish we knew why these things sometimes happen.'

'I'll bring you some tea,' said Laurel, after making her own inadequate attempts at consolation.

When the couple had recovered sufficiently to leave, she herself carried the baby tenderly to the mortuary, her own eyes awash with tears. It was the first cot death she had personally been involved with and it was a heart-breaking experience.

The department had almost emptied by the time she returned. Noticing Bruce Tyson in the corridor, she quickly made for the rest room to avoid meeting him. He was the last person she wanted to see when she was red of eyes and pink of nose. After tidying up she reported to the office.

'You go to lunch now, dear,' said Sister Maguire with a perceptive glance at Laurel's woebegone face.

Gratefully Laurel did so and in the canteen she met up with Dilys. 'I've had my fill of life's little dramas this morning,' she said, blowing her nose and sniffing.

Dilys was duly sympathetic, but she was never one to dwell on the seamy side of life. 'Well, you mustn't let it get to you. Cheer up! There's fun and frolics ahead. I suppose you haven't heard from our Paolo yet?'

'Rinaldo? No, why should I?'

Tucking into her sausage and mash, Dilys said, 'He's leaving today . . . he told me he was coming down to see you before he went. I've been giving him breathing exercises, he's a heavy smoker. And an outrageous bottom-pincher too,' she laughed. 'My seat's black and blue.'

Laurel managed a smile. 'He wasn't in a fit state to pinch mine, thank goodness.'

'You wait! He probably will,' Dilys prophesied.

Work in the department was less frantic in the afternoon, with mundane jobs such as removal of stitches, strapping sprained ankles, and dressings to be changed. Laurel's last patient was a Mr Smith with an angry swelling on the back of his neck.

'Mmm . . . that does look painful,' she murmured. 'Come with me and I'll find a doctor to see you.'

Leaving him in an examination bay, she went to the doctor's office. Andy Logan was not there, but she found Dr Moira Carp. 'An abscess? Oh God, I hate those messy things,' said Moira in a bored voice. 'Is it ripe for excision?'

'Looks like it to me,' said Laurel. 'He's in Room Three.'

Moira switched on her bedside smile for the patient's benefit. 'Hallo! Let's have a look at this, shall we?' She studied the red, shiny lump, pursing her shapely lips. 'Yes, I think we'd better open this up for you. All right, Mr Smith, we'll give you a shot of something to deaden the pain.'

Laurel took Mr Smith along to the treatment room where she helped him off with his jacket and tucked a disposable towel around his shoulders. She had the sterile Incision and Drainage pack ready when the doctor joined them.

With Lignocaine injected into the surrounding tissue, Moira prodded the site tentatively. 'Tell me if you can feel that?' On being assured that the area was quite numb she went ahead to make the inci-

sion, sitting on a chair to one side of him. 'Just
support his head, will you, Staff?'

Laurel rested Mr Smith's head against her protective plastic apron. As the scalpel went in, an
oozing mass spurted out all over her.

Moira's laugh tinkled out. 'So sorry about that,
Nurse. I'm glad it came your way and not mine!'

With a wry smile Laurel took a piece of gauze
from the trolley, cleaned off the offending mess and
dropped it into the soiled dressings bag. 'No good
being squeamish in this job, is it? Have you got the
core?'

'Not yet.' After some more probing the core
finally came away. 'I can pack it now,' said Moira.
'What have you got there . . . Eusol and paraffin?'

'Yes.' Laurel poured some of the solution into a
gallipot, in which the doctor soaked a strip of
ribbon gauze before feeding it into the cavity with
forceps.

'Just put a dressing over that for me, Nurse.'
Moira flashed her practised smile at Mr Smith
before leaving. 'Come in again tomorrow and we'll
clean it up for you.'

With the remaining patients all being attended
to, Laurel was preparing to go off duty when the
ebullient Mr Rinaldo descended upon her. He was
stylishly turned out in a lightweight pale blue suit
with a silky sheen to it. There was a chunky gold
chain around his neck and a heavy gold bracelet on
his wrist.

'Hallo, Mr Rinaldo. I heard you were going
home today. How are you?' She kept her rear well
out of reach.

'*Va bene!*' He threw his arms wide in an expansive gesture and gave her a dazzling smile, his dark eyes lustrous. 'Why you not come to see me? I ask where you are many times.'

'Well, my work is down here, not on the wards. But I didn't forget you . . . they told me you were getting on okay.'

'So I 'ave to come to find you . . . my special angel!' Rinaldo seized her hand and smothered her bare arm with kisses.

Laurel laughed and plunged her hands into the pockets of her uniform when he let her go. 'So take good care of yourself now, Mr Rinaldo. Don't go driving into any more lampposts.'

'Paolo, you call me Paolo, huh? Listen . . .' he went on effusively, 'I give a big party for all my kind friends, huh? I fix a date . . . everybody come.'

'Thank you, that would be lovely,' said Laurel. 'Now I really must go. 'Bye.' She disappeared into the staff room, smiling to herself.

'It's certainly nice to be appreciated,' she said later, going back to the house with Dilys. 'Expect he'll forget all about parties, though, once he gets back to normal.'

'Maybe. Maybe not,' mused Dilys. 'Did you dig the fancy gear and the Gucci shoes? He's not short of the ready, our Paolo.'

The girls let themselves into the darkening house. 'Em must be out,' Laurel said. 'Her half-day, wasn't it?'

'Yes. I hope she didn't go running after Phil again. She's still nuts about that swine, you know. And there's Mike Spring nuts about *her*. Always the way, isn't it, the people you go for don't go for you. Pity Mike's not a bit more pushy. I should imagine with him a girl would have to make most of the running. Gosh! I'm starving. What can we eat?'

'I bought a quiche from Marks . . . we can share that. I'll just go and take off my uniform.' Laurel ran upstairs.

Pausing on the landing, she noticed with some surprise that Emma's door was shut. Normally all their doors were left open until they went to bed. Something prompted her to knock and call, 'Em, you there?' Receiving no reply she opened the door. In the half-light she could see Emma sprawled on top of the bed, face down. 'Em?' she said anxiously, 'Are you all right?' There was no response. A shaft of fear went through her. Switching on the light she went over to the bed, her eyes falling upon empty packets of Panadol tablets and an empty glass on the bedside cabinet. She smelt the glass . . . whisky! And Emma was out cold!

Laurel ran to the top of the stairs, yelling: 'Dilys! Quick . . . I think Em's taken an overdose!'

She ran back to the bedroom, rolled the inert Emma over and shook her. 'Wake up, Em! Come on, wake up!'

Dilys took the stairs two at a time. 'My God!' she breathed, 'What do we do?'

'Better try walking her up and down,' panted Laurel.

Between them they managed to haul their friend to her feet, but it was no use. Emma just moaned and her legs sagged.

'We'll have to get her in for a washout!' Laurel raced downstairs, dialled 999, asked for the ambulance service and gave brief details.

At the hospital they sat around waiting and feeling helpless while the duty staff attended to Emma, washing out her stomach with warm water.

Presently Bob Merrick came out to see them. 'She'll be okay, girls. We've put her on a dextrose drip, and I'll get her warded for a few days. We'll have to keep her under obs for a bit.' He looked curious. 'She's not saying much. What's the trouble, love-life in a mess?'

'Might be,' Laurel said, guardedly. 'Thank God we found her when we did.' She sighed. 'I never want to live through another day like this.'

Bob looked from one to the other with a roguish grin. 'You birds should learn not to take life so seriously.'

'Oh, we all know *you* like to love and leave'em,' scoffed Dilys. 'You fellers have a lot to answer for.'

Later, when Emma had been transferred to the ward, they sat by her bedside for a while, trying to be supportive.

'Sorry to give you so much bother,' faltered Emma, biting trembling lips. 'I—I didn't actually plan to do it. I was feeling so cheesed off, thinking about Phil. I took a few pills trying to buck myself up . . . and I got a bit fuddled . . . s'pose I didn't realise how many I'd taken.'

'If only you'd talked to us!' Laurel said, 'It might have helped. It didn't dawn on me you were that desperate . . .'

'Well, it's all over now, and you've got to cut that

bastard right out of your life,' said Dilys. 'Plenty more fish in the sea.'

Emma gave a sad little smile. 'It'll be a long time before I let myself get involved with anyone else. Don't tell my folks, will you?' she said, looking worried. 'It'd only upset them.'

Her friends gave their word. 'We'll be in to see you again tomorrow, and I'll bring you a toothbrush and things,' promised Laurel as they left.

Pushing through the ward doors, they came face-to-face with Bruce Tyson on his way to check on one of his patients. News travels fast in a hospital and he paused to say, 'I heard about your friend. How is she?'

'She'll make it,' answered Dilys.

'What was her problem?' He glanced keenly from one to the other.

'A guy of course,' said Dilys pertly. 'Men are at the bottom of most problems, aren't they?'

Laurel couldn't have spoken if she'd tried. In his presence her own self-assurance wilted and a peculiar weakness affected her limbs. With his attention on Dilys for the moment, she was able to study him at leisure. There was no denying he was very fanciable. The deep-set blue eyes under those well-defined brows . . . the slight hollow in his cheeks . . . There was a kind of aura about him that commanded respect. Not a man to be crossed. She found herself wondering what kind of a lover he would be? Dynamic and forceful, no doubt. He did nothing by halves. He would demand complete surrender or nothing. And yet he'd had a failed marriage. Maybe the girl could not match up to his standards, she thought.

Suddenly the searching eyes honed in on hers. It was almost as though he could read her thoughts, and her colour rose.

'Love can be a source of great unhappiness. Don't you agree?' he said, speaking directly to Laurel.

She drew a long breath before answering. 'Everything has its highs and lows,' she returned in what she hoped was a cool voice.

The dark brows lifted expressively and he gave a short laugh. 'The oracle speaks! You'd better go to the top of the class.' With a cryptic smile he went on his way, leaving Laurel furious with herself that she had not come up with a clever reply to his sarcasm.

'Supercilious big-head!' she muttered. 'He always manages to put me down. Makes me feel like a five-year-old.'

Dilys giggled. 'I wouldn't mind being a five-year-old if he'd carry me up to bed.'

'Yes, I know what you mean,' said Laurel with a grin. 'That was a queer thing to say, wasn't it, about love being the cause of great unhappiness?'

'Maybe he's been crossed in love himself. Oh well, it's nice to know it cuts both ways and that men can be just as vulnerable as women.'

'Mmmm . . .' reflected Laurel, 'I think he's divorced. Perhaps he's still in love with her.'

The local church clock struck nine as they left the hospital grounds. They had still not eaten. 'I don't feel like going back and cooking now, do you?' said

Dilys. 'Let's grab something at the Fox and Hounds.'

The pub was a favourite haunt of the hospital staff. They were greeted by a number of people as they went to the bar, ordered chicken-in-a-basket and seated themselves at a table in the lounge.

Mike Spring sauntered over to join them, glass in hand. 'Hi! Emma not with you tonight?'

The news had evidently not caught up with him, but there was no point in trying to conceal it since it was bound to leak out sooner or later.

'She's been warded on Lister for the moment,' Dilys explained. 'Bit of a mix-up with some tablets she was taking . . . we had to rush her in for a washout.'

'It was quite unintentional,' put in Laurel staunchly.

There was genuine concern on Mike's round face. 'Oh, poor kid. Do you think . . . I mean, could I go and see her? Does she want visitors?'

'Sure, Mike, I expect she'd love to see you,' Dilys said. 'It would probably buck her up no end.'

'Right, I'll do that first chance I get.' He seemed really pleased to think they welcomed his suggestion.

Over the next few days both girls spent much of their off-duty with Emma and she made a good recovery. 'I'm having a week's sick-leave,' she told them, 'and Mike has offered to drive me home. Nice of him, isn't it?'

Laurel and Dilys exchanged knowing looks.

Emma smiled shyly. 'And you needn't go making anything of that, you two. He's just a nice bloke.'

Nevertheless, when they left Emma her friends agreed that perhaps things were going the right way for Mike. 'Looks like he's not so backward in coming forward after all,' remarked Laurel.

Dilys agreed. 'He's certainly seized his opportunity this time.'

With disaster averted Laurel went in to work the next day feeling on top of the world—until the disagreement which blew up between herself and Moira Carp. It was over a young woman brought in by her husband, her leg swathed in a wet tea-towel.

'She's scalded it rather badly,' he explained to Laurel.

The woman was clearly in great pain. Wheeling her to an examination room and helping her on to the bed, Laurel carefully removed the damp covering to look at the damage. She winced at the sight and extent of the area involved. 'However did you do this, Mrs Williams?'

'I had boiled up some nappies in a bucket,' she said, her lips quivering, 'then I climbed on a chair to get down a tin of baby food, and I stepped back into the bucket.'

Carefully Laurel replaced the covering to exclude the air before going to find a doctor. The only one unoccupied at the time was Moira. Laurel would have preferred Andy; she was not always too happy with Moira's judgment, but there was no choice.

Moira floated in, her white coat flapping over her

elegant pale blue skirt and cashmere sweater. She turned her honeyed smile on the patient and cast a casual eye over the scarlet flesh. It stretched from foot almost to knee. 'Hmm . . . Melolin dressings with some Flamazine should deal with that, Staff. She'd better come in again tomorrow for re-dressing, I suppose.' The doctor sauntered out again.

Laurel gazed after her in amazement. She could hardly believe her ears. 'I won't be a moment,' she said to Mrs Williams, and she hurried out to catch up with Moira in the corridor. 'Dr Carp,' she pointed out, 'that's a full circumference burn. It's going to be up in huge blisters before long . . . and she's quite shocked. Don't you think she should be referred?'

Moira frowned. 'No, I don't think so.' But she went back to take a second look. 'Oh well, perhaps I'd better put up a drip when you've finished the dressing. She can stay in the day ward for a couple of hours. Then there's no reason why she shouldn't go home.'

Laurel was troubled. She recognised the dangers of the blistering which would undoubtedly follow. With all-round damage such as this and nowhere for the fluid to spread, it could act as a tourniquet, cutting off circulation to the limb. In her own mind she felt the woman should be admitted, but what could Laurel do? It was not her place to refer a patient to the registrar.

Once more going after the doctor, she made a further attempt to reason with her. 'But it's full circumference,' she repeated. 'By tomorrow that leg will be in a critical condition. She's in no shape to go home really.'

They were outside the doctors' office. 'Don't argue with me, Nurse,' snapped Moira, although obviously a little less sure of herself.

To Laurel's embarrassment Bruce Tyson, emerging from the office at that moment, overheard part of their exchange. 'Problems?' he asked, with a shrewd glance from one to the other.

Moira switched on her smile. 'Oh, Bruce . . . if you can spare me a moment, I'd like your opinion on a patient.'

Laurel followed the doctors back into the examination room. Her pulse was racing while she watched the registrar's impassive features as he bent over the damaged leg, weighing up the severity of the injury.

It took him no time at all to come to a decision. Straightening up, he took Mrs Williams' hand in his, 'My dear, I think you'll have to go to our Burns Unit. That's a nasty leg you have there. You may need a skin graft.'

'That was my opinion,' lied Moira.

'You mean . . . I have to come in?' Mrs Williams' voice was tremulous. 'But I've got a young baby . . . and I'm still breast-feeding.'

'Don't worry,' Bruce said kindly, 'we can arrange to have your baby admitted with you. Is that your husband outside? I'll have a word with him.'

With a haughty glare at Laurel, Moira swept out after the registrar as he left the room.

Laurel smiled at the patient. 'Well, that's good.

I'm glad they've decided to take you in. It wouldn't have been easy for you at home.'

'Thank you, Nurse,' said Mrs Williams with a grateful sigh, 'I didn't really know how I was going to cope.'

That woman, Laurel fumed inwardly, *she's not fit to be a casualty officer*. And Moira had once against managed to take the credit for herself. It was lucky for the patient that Bruce had been on the spot. But what tale was Moira telling Bruce now? Laurel wondered.

Returning to the department after accompanying Mrs Williams to the Burns Unit, Laurel was called into the office by Sister Maguire. 'What's been going on between you and Dr Carp? She seems to be gunning for you.'

'Oh, I stuck my neck out on that patient's behalf.' Briefly she explained the situation. 'I should have felt awfully guilty if I'd let her send that poor woman home.'

Sister Maguire pursed her lips. 'I see. A tricky situation for you, but I don't think you need worry too much about what she may have said to Tyson. He's probably got Dr Carp taped by now, like the rest of us. That's not the first boob she's made, is it? Lucky for you her time's nearly up here. You're not going to be too popular with the lady.'

CHAPTER FIVE

PAOLO Rinaldo was as good as his word. Before the week was out an elaborately printed handbill appeared on the staff notice board at the Riversdale. It invited everyone to a Grand Fiesta in the ballroom of the Ristorante Rinaldo on Wednesday week, from nine until one a.m., free tickets to be obtained from the social secretary.

Personal invitations were received by all those who had been actively concerned with Rinaldo's recovery. Laurel's card came to the house accompanied by a bunch of long-stemmed red roses, in true Neapolitan style.

'Red roses, indeed!' smirked Dilys. 'That guy's fallen for you. Expect he can't wait to get you in a dark corner somewhere.'

They were in Emma's bedroom that Sunday morning, helping her pack to go home for her week's convalescence.

Sitting on the bed, swinging her legs, Laurel gave a soft chuckle. 'Then I shall have to make sure I keep away from dark corners. Honestly, I didn't think this party would come off. I mean, I know people are terribly grateful at the time, but they soon forget.'

'Oh, I thought he meant it.' Dilys sat on Emma's suitcase so that she could close it. 'Besides, he had something to be grateful for. Nearly a goner, wasn't he? If it hadn't been for that emergency trachy Tyson did in Re-sus . . .'

Moira's lapse on that particular occasion had filtered through the department.

'Seems like Bruce is always coming to your rescue,' put in Emma with a slow smile in Laurel's direction. 'He must be your guardian angel.'

'More like my pain in the neck!' said Laurel.

A ring at the front door interrupted their heart-to-heart. 'That sounds like your chauffeur, Em,' Dilys said. 'Get your coat on . . . I'll take your case down.'

Going to open the door, Laurel let Mike into the hall. 'Hallo. Em's just coming. Glad you're going with her, Mike. It'll be good for her to have company.'

He grinned self-consciously. 'Well, I did wonder if I was pushing my luck . . . but she seemed quite pleased I'd offered.'

He took the case from Dilys and beamed at Emma as she joined them. There was a fragility about her that made Laurel feel protective, but she was confident that Emma had a staunch champion in the steady, undemanding Mike.

Waving the pair of them goodbye, Dilys and Laurel stood on the doorstep and watched the car disappear. They went in and shut the door. 'Let's hope she's got that guy out of her system at last,' said Dilys.

'She did say that all this had helped her to get things into perspective,' Laurel reflected. 'She said she knew deep-down that Phil wasn't worth what she'd put herself through. Actually she and Mike would be well-suited, they're both gentle characters. But we mustn't matchmake. It's going to take her a while to get adjusted.'

Both girls were in thoughtful mood, discussing the effects that an overwhelming passion could have on one's life.

'At least she'll be able to lose herself in work until she feels like integrating again. Neuro-surgery must be quite absorbing.' Dilys paused as the telephone rang and she went to answer it. 'Hallo? Oh, hi, Andy. Yes, we're both here. No . . . we're not doing anything special. Just a minute . . .' She put her hand over the mouthpiece and turned to Laurel. 'Andy's taking Ahmed Singh to see the Cutty Sark. He wants to know if we'll make up a four?'

'Love to,' agreed Laurel.

Ahmed was an Asian houseman whom Andy seemed to have taken under his wing. He was an extremely polite and well-spoken fellow with a perpetual twinkle in his brown eyes. Everyone liked Ahmed.

Some thirty minutes later the boys picked them up. Piling into Andy's rather ancient white Dolomite, they made for Greenwich where the famous old tea-clipper had its last resting place in dry-dock. They were all in carefree mood as they drove through a park bright with spring flowers, emerging at the far end into the by-ways of the historic town.

Searching for a place to leave the car, at the end of a narrow side-street they caught a glimpse of the intricately-rigged sailing ship, its towering masts dwarfing the surrounding shabby buildings.

'There she is!' exclaimed Andy. 'Now that's what I call a ship.'

'Looks romantic,' laughed Laurel, 'but I bet modern ships are a darn sight more comfortable. There's a car park this way.' She pointed him in the direction of the gravelled site that Bruce had carried her across the day that she had lost her heel.

'They don't let people aboard before two o'clock,' Andy remembered, 'so we may as well grab a pub lunch first.'

He led the way to an ancient inn he knew of, where they gathered around a small oak table and ate crusty bread and cheese and pickles in the low-ceilinged, black-beamed saloon-bar. Conversation was light-hearted and easy between them all. Dilys and Andy constantly struck sparks off each other, but Laurel sensed that underlying the teasing was a mutual attraction. So that's how the land lies! she thought, with a secret smile. Dilys and Andy . . . well, well!

Laurel concentrated her attention on Ahmed, listening attentively while he told her all about his plans to go back to India to work among his own people. 'I'm just waiting for my FRCP results. My second attempt,' he admitted with a rueful grin.

'Oh well, lots of people have to take it a number of times, don't they?' consoled Laurel. 'How long have you been over here, Ahmed?'

'I went to school here . . . and then on to Cambridge. I am to be married when I go back home.' He reached into the pocket of his windcheater and showed her a photo of a dark-eyed beauty in an elaborate sari.

'She's lovely,' said Laurel. 'Well, let's hope you've passed this time.'

Andy downed the last of his lager. 'Drink up, you two, it's time we got going.'

Following his example, they were soon joining the small queue of people waiting to be shown over the old sailing vessel. The guide pointed out the cramped quarters and primitive living conditions that had been the lot of nineteenth-century sailors and, after reciting his spiel, left them free to explore on their own. The musty museum below decks held a motley collection of colourful ships' figureheads. It was full of atmosphere with old engravings and relics of maritime life as it once was.

After clambering up and down steep companionways the friends emerged once more into the sunlight.

'What shall we do now?' said Andy as they returned to the quayside. 'Do you want to trail round the Maritime Museum, or shall we take a launch up the Thames to Charing Cross Pier?'

It was beautifully warm for early May. 'It'll be great on the river,' said Laurel. 'Let's do that.'

'Right, everybody? This way to the landing stage.' Andy sauntered ahead with his arm around Dilys' shoulders. Ahmed and Laurel followed. They were approaching the smaller dry-dock where *Gipsy Moth* was moored, when Andy pointed and called, 'Look who's here!'

Laurel's pulse quickened as Andy and Dilys went over to where a tall man and a small boy were in rapt contemplation of Sir Francis Chichester's famous craft. There was no mistaking the set of those broad shoulders and the back of that classic head on its strong neck.

'Oh, it's Bruce!' exclaimed Ahmed, going to join them. She had no alternative but to follow.

Andy ruffled the youngster's wealth of dark brown hair. 'Hallo there, young David. Managed to prise your dad away from work, have you?'

The boy nodded with a roguish grin. It had the same endearing quality that made Laurel feel defenceless on the rare occasions when Bruce smiled. So there was a child, she mused in some surprise. She wondered who had custody of the boy. Perhaps he lived with his mother and Bruce saw him when he could. She understood a little better that remark of his about the unhappiness that love could cause. It must be hell, she thought, when your family disintegrated.

Bruce was relaxed and affable now, exchanging pleasantries with them and talking about ships. 'We're on our way to see the *Cutty Sark*,' he said. 'David is doing a project about ships at school.'

'We've just come from there.' Andy winked at David. 'You want to get your dad to buy you a model in a bottle. Well, we're going for a trip on the Thames now. Cheers! Enjoy your day.'

'I didn't know he had a son,' remarked Dilys when they had parted company. 'He lives in the residents' quarters, doesn't he? Where's his wife?'

'Sad story,' Andy told them. 'She drowned in a holiday boating accident, so I heard. The kid lives with Bruce's parents at Tonbridge.'

His wife was dead? So *that* was the mystery of his marriage and the reason for his Tonbridge trips.

Laurel felt a stab of remorse that she had been misjudging the man. He had talked about bereavement affecting people in many different ways. Undoubtedly he spoke from personal experience. You never really knew what made people the way they were, she pondered. Her thoughts wavered between pity for Bruce and pity for the child at having to be separated from his father for much of the time.

They were approaching the pier and Andy urged them to hurry. 'Step on it, there's a boat in,' he said.

Getting a move on, they were just in time to board the motor-launch before it set off downriver.

Over the tannoy the captain delivered his commentary on things of interest on the way. Disused warehouses and derelict wharves sat idly on the banks of the sun-dappled river which was busy with craft of various kinds. Presently they were passing under picturesque Tower Bridge with the grey bulk of the Tower of London on their right. Then on past *HMS Discovery* of Captain Scott and Antarctic fame, to berth at Charing Cross Pier.

All London seemed on holiday that mild May Sunday. The Victoria Embankment thronged with sightseers and amateur photographers. Ahmed bought ice-creams from a riverside stall and they leaned over the parapet by Cleopatra's Needle, watching the gulls swoop and soar.

'"Sweet Thames, run softly till I end my song",' quoted Dilys dreamily, between licks of her cone.

Strains of a military band drifted over to them

from the Embankment Gardens. Crossing the road, they stretched out on the grass, listening to the music, exchanging small-talk and laughing a lot until Ahmed reminded them that he was on call that night and ought to get back.

Taking the launch back to Greenwich, they picked up Andy's car, dropped Ahmed off at the hospital and returned to the house.

They were all hungry, a day in the fresh air having sharpened their appetites. 'Come on then, what have you got in the cupboard?' Andy breezed.

'Not much,' said Laurel. She searched the fridge and produced two tomatoes, three eggs, two sausages and some cold potatoes.

'Right, leave it to me. I'm expert with the frying-pan.' He tied a tea-towel round his jeans and went to work.

Dilys found a can of baked beans and put them on to heat. Laurel made coffee, and all three sat at the kitchen table and ate heartily.

'You two go and relax in the other room,' Laurel said afterwards. 'I'll do the washing-up. Then if you don't mind I'll have to disappear. I'm in block all next week and there are some notes I ought to read up.' After cleaning up in the kitchen she discreetly went to her room to give Dilys and Andy some privacy.

Switching on her transistor, she got out her course notes and tried to concentrate on things like Microbiology and Control of Infection.

But it was difficult to stop her mind from wandering and going back over the events of the day. Bruce and his son kept creeping into her thoughts.

He had seemed an engaging youngster. She wondered what would happen to the child should Bruce decide to marry again. Someone like Moira Carp, for instance. She shuddered at the idea of Moira in the role of stepmother.

Sighing, Laurel finally gave up the attempt to study, ran herself a bath, splashed in her favourite bath oil and indulged her tired limbs before turning in.

The following morning she joined Dilys for breakfast in the kitchen. During study block her hours were from nine until four-thirty. As a physiotherapist Dilys always worked regular hours.

'It's nice to join the ranks of the privileged for a change,' Laurel said, feeling pleasantly relaxed in her jeans and a loose cream sweater, since they were not required to wear uniform during teaching sessions. Although mentally demanding, the break came as a welcome interlude from the sometimes hectic pace and traumas of the department.

Dilys stifled a yawn as she buttered a piece of toast. 'I'm shattered. Don't think fresh air agrees with me.'

Laurel grinned. 'It's not the fresh air . . . it's burning the midnight oil with Andy! I didn't know you fancied him?'

'Good. I'm glad I wasn't that obvious. He thinks it's all his idea.'

After finishing their meal and piling the crocks in the sink, the two girls set off together, going their own ways at the hospital.

For Laurel the day started with a get-together of the six post-graduate staff nurses with their clinical tutor. Over coffee they had a résumé of the week's programme to be followed before proceeding to their first assignment, a lecture on the nervous system from the neurological registrar.

The week passed busily with further lectures from surgical and medical staff, outside visits to specialised departments in other hospitals and educational films produced by various drug houses on the latest equipment and treatments. Joining ward rounds with consultants and their firms, it was interesting to renew acquaintance with some of the patients who had passed through their hands on A and E. In the children's ward Laurel came across young Robin, her appendix patient, and she was glad to find him making good progress.

There were also working lunches in the lecture room when available medical staff dropped in to talk about matters in their own particular fields. At the seminar on the last Friday lunchtime Bruce Tyson was there, along with paediatrician Chris Goodman. Between the wine and cheese they all discussed surgical emergencies, child abuse and battered babies.

As the meeting broke up Bruce singled out Laurel to enquire after her father.

'Oh, he's getting on fine, thank you. He came home yesterday. I'm going down to see him when we finish this evening.'

'I'm going that way again myself,' he said. 'I'll take you.'

The offer took her by surprise. 'Well, thanks all the same, but there's no need. My own car is fixed now.'

His eyebrows lifted. 'You'll be coming back on Sunday evening, presumably?'

She nodded.

'Then there's little point in wasting two lots of petrol. I'll pick you up around six.'

Without waiting for her agreement or refusal, he walked off in the company of Chris Goodman. Laurel gritted her teeth with annoyance. 'The cool cheek of that man,' she complained to Kathie, 'changing my plans without so much as a by-your-leave!'

Kathie Moran looked intrigued. 'Perhaps he likes your company?'

Laurel made a doubtful face. 'I should hardly think so. He's probably just throwing his weight about.'

Their final afternoon teaching session was a film on cardiac arrest and resuscitation methods, followed by discussion.

After finishing up with tea and iced buns in the canteen with her fellow staff nurses, Laurel drove home to pack for the weekend and await the arrival of her self-appointed driver.

Dilys returned at the same time as the Rover drew up outside. 'The big white chief's come for you,' she told Laurel. 'I asked him in, but he said you'd be quicker if he waited outside. Getting to be a habit this, isn't it? You'll be finding yourselves talked about. Moira will be gunning for you more than ever.'

'I'd be doing him a favour if I came between them,' said Laurel darkly. 'But don't get the idea he's at all interested in me. It is sensible, I suppose, to take one car since we're both going in the same direction and coming back at the same time. Do you think I should offer to share the petrol?'

'Don't be crazy,' laughed Dilys. 'He'd probably be insulted if you did.'

'Well, I hate being indebted to him.' Laurel put on her jacket, said goodbye and went out to where Bruce sat waiting. He pushed open the door for her and she slipped in beside him, throwing her overnight bag into the back.

'Thank you,' she said, sinking into the luxury of the fawn leather upholstery. 'This'll be a more comfortable ride than in my old bone-shaker.'

'Belt up, then . . . unless you want to shoot through the windscreen when I step on the brakes.'

Obediently she fastened her seat-belt. The car purred into action.

It was still light as they wove their way through the suburbs and out into the Kent countryside. Trees and hedgerows were in the full glory of new spring growth. The scent of hawthorn hung on the air and now and then Laurel glimpsed the soft sheen of bluebells through shady woods. It gave her a sense of well-being.

Making an attempt at light conversation, she said: 'What did your little boy think of the *Cutty Sark*? I used to hate having to write essays after visiting places.'

'Oh, I made a few notes for him. At his age he'd rather be kicking a ball about than doing homework. He's not too academically inclined yet.'

She glanced at him sideways. 'I suppose that's

what makes you good with youngsters, having one of your own.'

'Good with youngsters, am I?' His mouth twitched. 'Personally I don't rate myself very high in the parental stakes. I don't even provide a permanent home for the lad.'

'We-ell, I suppose that would be difficult for you in the circumstances.'

'I'm flattered you can make allowances for me. Perhaps you could work out a neat solution?' There was a provoking patronage in his voice. 'But then, my problems are hardly your concern. Let's talk about you. What are you going to do when your time's up at the Riversdale?'

'I'll apply for a sister's post somewhere, I expect.'

'You'll probably get married before long, and that will be another good vocation gone to waste.'

She glared at him. 'Are you the sort who thinks a woman's place is in the kitchen?'

He suppressed a smile. 'Oh, I'm not against emancipation, but some women are more suited to that than others. I can picture you with a brood at your heels.'

'Can you!' she returned tartly, 'Well, I'm not quite ready to bury myself in domesticity yet.'

'Nobody is ever quite ready. It's something that creeps up on you.'

'Nothing and no one creeps up on me undetected.'

'Fully in control, are we?' he said with a superior smile.

'Yes!' She gazed straight ahead, furious with

herself for finding him attractive in spite of his overbearing attitude.

As they neared her destination she directed him to her father's house. It was a solid red-brick detached residence, fronted by a circular drive around a lawn bordered with tulips. There was no brass plate at the front gates.

'Your father doesn't have his surgery here, then?' Bruce asked, turning into the drive and bringing the car to a halt opposite the front door.

'No, it's a group practice in the town. Well, thanks for the lift.' She alighted and somewhat to her surprise, he followed suit, stretching his arms lazily above his head and saying, 'I think it's time I paid my respects to your father. He might like to satisfy himself on the company you keep.'

She took her bag from the back seat. 'He's not in the habit of checking up on me . . . but if you must . . .'

He followed her to the house. Before she had time to ring the bell the door opened, and standing in the hallway behind her father she saw the stalwart figure of Gary, her ex-boyfriend. He looked his usual virile self; crinkly fair hair in casual disorder, skin tanned, muscled legs encased in jeans. But she had no feelings of regret at having parted from him, just surprise at seeing him there as he grinned at her over her father's shoulder.

Dr Swann embraced his daughter affectionately. Gary proceeded to do likewise, taking her in a bearhug and giving her an unnecessarily prolonged kiss on the mouth.

Extremely put out at this display in front of

Bruce, she pulled away, her colour heightened.

'Daddy, this is Bruce Tyson, our senior surgical registrar,' she said. 'He brought me down to the clinic to see you, remember?'

'Ah, yes. Most kind of you.' The two men shook hands.

'. . . and this is Gary Grantham, the son of Dad's partner,' Laurel explained to Bruce.

'How d'you do.' Bruce extended his hand and Gary took it. The two eyed each other critically.

'Do come in!' Dr Swann ushered their guest into the living-room. 'Will you have a drink?'

'Thank you,' said Bruce. 'Just a small one.'

'If you'll excuse me a moment,' said Laurel, 'I'd better go and say hallo to Jonesy.' She left them and went in search of her father's housekeeper.

Mrs Jones was in the kitchen preparing dinner. She had been with the family since before Laurel's mother died and she greeted Laurel with genuine pleasure. 'Hallo, dear. Lovely to see you again. And isn't it great to have your dad back on his feet?'

Laurel smiled. 'It certainly is. Quite a shock, wasn't it, him getting sick. I thought he was indestructible. How do you think he seems now?'

'Very well, considering. His digestion's a bit delicate, but Miss Ingrid is keeping her eye on him. You'll be seeing her tomorrow, I expect.' She chatted on, finishing off the salad she was arranging. 'It's cold chicken tonight since I didn't know what time you would get here, and there's a jam sponge with custard for afters. You don't mind serving it, do you? Only I have to be going, I promised to babysit for my daughter.'

'Yes, you push off as soon as you like,' Laurel said, 'I'll see to everything.'

'Right, I'll go then.' Mrs Jones hung up her apron and put on her coat. Laurel went with her to see her out of the front door.

Gary came out into the hall as she was about to go back into the kitchen. 'I didn't expect to find you here,' she said, a trifle frigidly.

'No, I don't suppose you did,' he put on a contrite expression, 'not after that stupid letter I wrote. You didn't answer it?'

'Did you expect me to? There was nothing more to say.'

'There is now.' He put his hands on her shoulders and looked into her face. 'Sweetheart . . . I owe you an apology. Was there ever such a clot as me? That other affair, it was only a flash in the pan. A ghastly mistake. Forgive me?'

Laurel gave a short laugh. 'Who's been getting at you, your dad? There's really nothing to forgive, Gary,' she went on, softening. 'It wouldn't have happened if you'd . . . if we'd really loved each other.'

He gave her a little shake. 'Oh, come on now. Don't be like that. I *do* love you . . . I just got sidetracked by this sex symbol. Back to square one, eh?'

Compared with the man who had driven her down, Gary seemed so immature, a mere boy in spite of his manly physique. She shook her head regretfully. 'No, you were right the first time. We weren't truly in love, Gary. I am fond of you, but not in that way. It was other people expected it of us. We can still be friends, can't we?'

'Darling, I *do* love you,' he insisted. 'You'll never find anyone who'll love you as much as I do.'

Laurel shrugged. 'I'm sorry . . . it's over for me . . . burned out.'

He scowled and jerked his head towards the living-room. 'Is it that guy in there?'

'No! Why has it got to be anybody?'

'Why else would he go to the trouble of driving you down?'

'His parents happen to live this way, that's why. He was only being accommodating.'

'Huh!' Gary exclaimed. 'If you believe that, you'll believe anything.'

'Oh, don't be ridiculous.'

The door of the living-room opened and Bruce and her father appearing on the scene put an end to further argument.

'I invited him to stay to dinner,' Laurel's father said, 'but I couldn't persuade him. Another time perhaps.'

'It's been a pleasure to meet you, sir,' said Bruce with a smile. 'Goodbye,' he said politely to Gary, and turning towards Laurel, 'I'll see *you* on Sunday, about eight. Enjoy your weekend!' The irony in his voice clearly indicated that he thought Gary had claims on her. Well, he could think what he liked, she thought crossly. It was none of his business.

Soon after Bruce left, Gary also departed in something of a huff. 'What's biting that young man?' asked Dr Swann with a shrewd glance at his daughter.

'Oh, he wanted to start things up again between us, but I didn't want to.'

He put an arm around her shoulders, his eyes twinkling. 'Can I guess why?'

'No, you can't,' she laughed. 'And just because you've decided to get yourself hitched don't try and mix it for me. I'll bring in the meal.' Giving him a swift peck on the cheek, she went back to the kitchen.

Ingrid came over for dinner the following day and there was much talk of their plans for the future. The wedding date had been fixed for mid-June, which would give Dr Swann time to recuperate.

'He's going to have to take life much more easily after this,' declared Ingrid. 'He shouldn't do night calls any more.'

'You're not putting me out to grass yet,' protested Dr Swann with a chuckle. 'But perhaps I will slow up a little. We've been talking about taking on a younger partner anyway. That's something we shall have to get down to.' Sitting beside Ingrid on the sofa, he patted her hand.

They made a handsome couple, Laurel thought, and she was glad that things were working out for them.

On Sunday she had her father to herself. She saw to it that he took his medication and enjoyed generally fussing over him. In the afternoon he sat in the garden in the sun while she pottered about doing some weeding and spraying the roses. Later she brought out tea for them and they watched the blue-tits flying in and out of the nesting-box in the old apple tree.

'I was ten when you put that up,' Laurel remembered, her mind going back over the years.

'Yes. You do know, darling, that our plans are going to make no difference to you, don't you? This will always be your home. Ingrid is very fond of you.'

'I'll be a sister to her,' grinned Laurel. 'We shall get on fine, don't worry.'

'And I expect you'll be setting up a home of your own one of these days.'

She wrinkled her nose at him. 'Stop trying to marry me off. I'm in no hurry.'

Promptly at eight that evening Bruce arrived to drive her back. He came in to have a coffee before they set out. Laurel could tell that he had made a favourable impression on her father who was inclined to be short with people of whom he didn't approve. Their conversation, quite naturally, turned to professional matters and they would have gone on talking indefinitely had not Laurel pointed out that time was getting on.

It was ten-thirty before she and Bruce were on the road. The night air was soft and scented, the sky star-studded, making her feel at peace with herself and everyone.

'Your father seems to have made a good recovery,' Bruce remarked.

'Yes, he does, doesn't he? Did you have a good weekend?'

'Mmm,' he said equivocally. 'David's grandparents are inclined to spoil him, but I'm hardly in a position to criticise.'

She agreed. 'And anyway, you wouldn't want to play the heavy father when you do see him.'

'Is that how you see me, in the rôle of heavy father?' he growled. It was almost as though he wanted to pick a fight with her.

'I expect you could be,' she returned levelly.

'A parent does have responsibilities. But you wouldn't know about that.'

'A bit of spoiling does no harm,' Laurel remarked. 'I expect your parents are only trying to compensate for what David is missing in other ways.'

'You don't need to remind me.'

'Pardon me for breathing!' she said.

They drove in silence for a while, the atmosphere tense between them. She watched the red tail-lights of the traffic ahead of them, wishing she had not reacted to his bad temper. In the light of her new knowledge about his past she had meant to make an effort to be agreeable. So much for good intentions.

Presently he said, 'When are you going to stop sulking?'

'I'm not sulking. I'm merely trying not to put my foot in it again. You do seem to be a bit touchy in some areas.'

'Getting crotchety in my old age, eh?'

'How old is that?'

'Thirty-eight. And you are?'

'Twenty-four.'

'My goodness! No wonder I seem like the heavy parent!'

'Well, there's no need to behave like one with me,' snapped Laurel.

The air crackled with animosity. 'That hefty young Romeo who greeted you so passionately when we came down on Friday, where does he fit into your scheme of things?' Bruce threw at her.

'It wasn't passion. It was friendship. We've known each other a long time.'

'That was friendship?' His mouth twisted wryly. 'I suggest you wake up to the facts of life, young lady, and stop bestowing your favours so indiscriminately.'

His censorious tone of voice made her see red. 'And I suggest you mind your own business. Don't talk to me like a two-year-old. Your authority stops at the hospital gates, remember?'

He replied by switching on the radio. 'You made me love you' sang the doleful voice of an old-time music hall artiste. 'And that's hardly appropriate, is it?' He retuned the set to an orchestral station.

At last they drew up outside her house. 'Thank you,' she said in tight little voice.

He drummed on the wheel with his fingers without looking at her. 'My pleasure.'

'Liar!' Gathering her things together, she scrambled out of the car and slammed the door. He drove away immediately.

Letting herself into the house, Laurel was relieved to find she had the place to herself. She didn't feel like talking to anyone. She was as wound up as a tight spring. She could have screamed with vexation. Making a coffee she took it up to her room. 'Oh, get lost, Bruce Tyson!' she muttered to herself. And then, for no accountable reason, her eyes filled with tears.

CHAPTER SIX

BACK on duty the following day Laurel was greatly relieved that Bruce did not put in an appearance on A and E. He exasperated her beyond reason and yet there was something almost obsessional about her growing preoccupation with the man.

But it became impossible for her to avoid contact with him altogether with his presence being required in the department on later occasions. His manner towards her, while being politely professional, was pointedly aloof. She responded similarly, restricting her remarks to matters concerning patients, keeping her personal feelings well under control despite the disturbing effect he had upon her.

It was on the Wednesday of Rinaldo's party that their display of indifference cracked. Towards the end of Laurel's span of duty Bob Merrick had to call the registrar to examine a heavy-weight lady with a ruptured varicose vein.

'Yes, I think surgery is the only answer here,' Bruce agreed. 'We'll need to strip that vein for you.' He gave the patient a disarming smile and made arrangements for her admission.

Accompanying her to the ward, Laurel exchanged glances with Kathie Moran who appeared to be having some difficulty in persuading a mentally-retarded woman towards the treatment room.

Returning some ten minutes later, Laurel was startled to see a kidney dish come hurtling out into the corridor. It was followed by a jugful of solution and the sounds of shrill protests and crashing equipment. She hurried to see if she could help as Bruce also shot from an adjoining room to investigate.

Laurel saw Kathie's glasses go flying as she and the registrar struggled to control the frenzied patient. The woman was lashing out with almost superhuman strength at everything and everyone within reach. The dressings trolley overturned with a clatter.

'Get the police!' Bruce barked at Laurel, trying to restrain the flailing arms.

She ran to obey, alerting Sister Maguire and a porter as well. Between them they had managed to sedate the patient by the time two officers arrived to take charge.

With order restored, Sister shepherded Kathie to the coffee room to calm her down, while Laurel stayed behind to clear up the wreckage.

'Thanks for your help,' Bruce said, breathing heavily as he picked up his stethoscope from the floor and smoothed back his dishevelled hair. He examined the torn pocket of his white coat and Laurel saw that one of his hands was deeply gouged and bleeding.

'That looks nasty. Can I clean it up for you?'

'If you like.' He perched on a stool amid the chaos.

She found a gallipot and poured in some Savlon solution. A tremor went down her spine as she took his large, strong hand in hers and carefully swabbed the lacerations before putting a plaster over the worst of them.

'Nicely done.' There was a wicked gleam in the keen blue eyes. 'Do you think I should be admitted?'

She turned away and began to pick up some of the scattered equipment. 'To a psychiatric ward, possibly,' she retorted.

He glowered and strode away.

One up to me! she thought, wrinkling her nose at his departing back, reluctantly admiring the leonine grace of his long limbs.

It was nine-thirty before she was home. On the hall table there was a scribbled note from Dilys to say that she and Andy had gone ahead to the party. 'Take a taxi and we'll bring you home' she wrote.

Laurel decided to do that and booked a taxi to pick her up in half an hour. She then took a quick shower before getting dressed for the evening, deciding on her filmy black chiffon with the ribbon shoulder straps. It highlighted to perfection her creamy shoulders and she knew she looked good as she added a silver rope-chain around her neck and put on silver sandals. Her tumble of nutbrown curls needed little grooming beyond a light brushing. A touch of eye shadow, a smear of lip gloss, a dash of her favourite perfume and she was ready to enjoy herself.

Arriving at the restaurant, Laurel handed in her fur jacket to the cloakroom attendant, took a brief reassuring glance in the mirror and went to join the company.

The festivities were in full swing, a hubbub of

chatter and laughter arising above the music in the softly-lit hall. Rinaldo's ballroom, which he let out for private parties, weddings and such occasions, was capable of holding around eighty guests and tonight his party was well supported. The lavishly decorated room was bordered by small floodlit alcoves with murals depicting Italian scenes— Venetian gondolas, orange groves, views of Capri and Mount Vesuvius. Tables were scattered around the perimeter with lighted red candles flickering in silver candelabra on snowy cloths. At one end of the room was the bar, and at the other a low platform to accommodate the three-piece band of guitar, electric keyboard and drums.

Making her way past dancing couples, Laurel exchanged greetings with a few people while she looked for Dilys and Andy. When the music ceased she caught sight of them approaching one of the tables and went over to join them.

'Hi!' said Andy, 'What can I get you, Laurel?'

'Dry Martini, please.' Bright-eyed, she seated herself alongside Dilys on one of the comfortable red padded chairs.

Rinaldo had spotted her arrival and came bounding over to greet her. He was exquisitely groomed in a maroon velvet jacket, tightly fitting black trousers and an embroidered white shirt. 'So 'ere you are at last!' he said, his dark eyes glowing, taking her hand and kissing it gallantly. 'I think you never come!'

'Well, I didn't get off until quite late,' Laurel explained with an apologetic smile.

He beamed at her. 'You miss nothing. We serve

the buffet now you are 'ere, huh? Then you dance with Paolo . . . I come back later.' He went away to give his orders.

Dilys gave Laurel a knowing look. 'Watch it! He's got it bad.'

Laurel laughed. 'Well, he can hardly seduce me in a roomful of people, and I'm coming home with you, aren't I?'

The music started up again and Ahmed appeared at her elbow to ask for a dance.

'You seem to be in good spirits tonight, Ahmed,' she said, noting an air of buoyancy about him. 'Had some good news?'

'Yes. I've received my results . . . and I've passed.'

'Oh! That's wonderful . . . I am glad.' Impulsively she planted a kiss on his smooth brown cheek. 'There'll be no stopping you now, I suppose? You'll be catching the next plane home.'

'Well, not quite so quickly as that. I have to finish my time at the Riversdale first.' He chatted on blithely about his plans.

Dancing came to an end and a team of waiters carrying silver trays shoulder-high marched into the hall to set refreshments on the tables. There was a well-presented assortment of hors d'oeuvres, vol-au-vents, dainty sandwiches, asparagus tips, chicken legs and pizza, accompanied by red or white wine. Paolo had stinted nothing. He even put on some entertainment while they ate, in the shape of a couple in colourful costume dancing a tarantella. Caught up in the lively atmosphere, Laurel joined with others in clapping to the rhythm.

Her glance was suddenly drawn to the next table, where Sister Helen Bates from ITU had been joined by Bruce Tyson. A quiver ran through her as their eyes met and he raised his glass in unsmiling acknowledgment. Casually she returned the salute. It surprised her to see him there. She concluded that Rinaldo must have sent him a personal invitation. Determined not to let his brooding presence spoil her evening, she turned her attention back to her companions.

When dancing began again Paolo presented himself before Laurel with a courtly bow. She rose and smiled and went into his outstretched arms. Holding her intimately he nuzzled his cheek against hers. 'I begin to think you will not come,' he murmured huskily, 'and I give my party specially for you, *cara mia.*'

'Oh, come on,' she returned with a light laugh. 'Who are you kidding? Still, the roses were lovely . . . thank you.'

'Beautiful flowers for a beautiful lady. Now you are 'ere, and I am 'appy.' His warm lips teased the lobe of her ear. 'Mmmm . . . you smell delightful.'

Laurel was begining to get rather worried by his ardent manner. He had a sensual way of dancing, one slim muscular leg forcing its way between hers, almost throwing her off-balance. His breath was hot on her neck, his hand feeling around her buttocks. Pointedly she moved the hand to her waist and attempted to put more space between them.

'You not like Paolo?' he enquired mournfully.

'Of course I do . . . but I don't like being pawed in public.'

'Ah!' he nodded in understanding. 'The English reserve, huh? Later we find some place more private and I teach you how to love.' He pulled her close again and dropped a light kiss on her nose.

She giggled, not taking him too seriously. 'I don't need any lessons in love. Besides, I have a boyfriend,' she fibbed. 'He'd probably black your eye if he could see you.'

'And I punch 'im too,' declared Paolo with comic ferocity.

The music stopped and he escorted her back to her friends. '*Scusi* . . . but I 'ave some business to see to. I come back for you later, huh?'

Laurel was disconcerted to find that in her absence their table had been pushed together to join forces with Helen and the registrar.

'Hallo!' she said, a trifle breathlessly, when Bruce rose to offer her a seat. 'You didn't say you were coming tonight.'

He eyed her with disapproval. 'You didn't ask. And since you appear to be taken up with the attentions of our host, I should imagine my appearance is of little consequence,' he said in a chilling undertone.

She gritted her teeth in annoyance. 'Why can't you stop picking on me? I can't help it if he gets carried away.'

His lips curled. 'It probably depends on how much encouragement he receives.'

'He got no encouragement from me, but I could hardly make a scene when it's his party. Anyway, he does have a certain charm.' She waved a careless hand, 'It's quite touching, putting all this on for us out of gratitude.'

'Touching seems to be the operative word in his case. If you play with fire, expect to get burned.'

'I'm not a complete beginner.' With a frosty smile she removed herself to the other end of the table where Dilys, Andy and Ahmed were seated.

The music restarted and Andy and Dilys got up to dance. Ahmed excused himself, saying, 'I'd better have this one with Helen.'

Glancing up, Laurel caught sight of the eager-eyed Paolo making a beeline in her direction again. She looked around for escape and caught Bruce's eye. 'Will you come to my rescue?' she asked in desperation. 'I'd rather not tangle with Paolo at the moment.'

He rose and took her onto the floor. 'Playing hard to get?'

'No . . . but you warned me against encouraging him. Trust you to misinterpret my actions.'

She was not surprised to find him a good dancer. He was easy to follow, guiding her with a firm hold, but the touch of his vital body against hers made her legs feel oddly inadequate.

'So you think you're ready for the advanced class now, do you?' he said presently, looking down at her with searching eyes.

Her heart thumped as she gave him stare for stare. 'The advanced class? Why, have you been taking lessons?'

His grip on her tightened disturbingly. 'What are you asking for, a demonstration?' Without warning he pulled her into a shadowy alcove, took her chin in his hands and laid his mouth over hers, fiercely demanding. 'How's that for starters?'

Laurel's eyes blazed as he released her. 'Oh! H-how dare you!' she gasped.

'Foreigners don't hold all the aces,' he retorted smoothly. 'Ahmed, or Paolo, or Bruce . . . now you've sampled them all you'll be in a better position to judge, won't you?'

Her mouth gaped. Surely he wasn't accusing her of having an affair with Ahmed. He must have jumped to conclusions on seeing her congratulatory kiss. She would have slapped his face if only she'd dared . . . but she wouldn't have put it past him to retaliate in kind. She relieved her feelings by saying, 'You really are insufferable. Perhaps you're jealous?'

'Cradle-snatching is not my style,' he scoffed. 'Now if you'll excuse me, I have to go. I'll leave you to your adolescent games.' Taking her by the elbow he propelled her back to the table.

His imperturbable calm made her so angry she could have exploded. She watched him make his way over to Rinaldo and shake hands with him, most correctly, before disappearing. Mad though she was, his departure left her feeling desolate. 'Hateful brute', she muttered and, almost on the verge of tears, she went to the cloakroom to compose herself.

With the wine flowing freely the night's festivities continued with a swing. Paolo diplomatically shared his favours around and when next he danced with Laurel his behaviour was more discreet. 'I think I go too fast for you, huh?' he said apologetically, 'but I cannot 'elp how I feel. One day you will let Paolo love you, yes?'

'No!' returned Laurel with a light laugh. She couldn't continue to be cross with him. In spite of his pressing ways he was a likeable character and amusing to be with.

'You wait for me and I take you 'ome?' he suggested when the party came to an end.

'Thanks all the same, Paolo, but I'm going with friends.'

'Then I ring you tomorrow, *cara mia*, and we make the date, huh?'

'We'll see,' she hedged, not wanting to give offence after his generosity. 'Thanks for the lovely evening.'

Going back to the house with Dilys and Andy, she chatted with them for a while over coffee before taking herself up to bed.

In the solitude of her room Laurel sighed as she hung up her dress. What a great evening it would have been but for her flare-up with Bruce. She felt utterly deflated. There was Dilys, her romance with Andy obviously making great strides, and Emma was being pursued by the devoted Mike, while her own love-life seemed to be in the doldrums. True, there was Paolo making all the right noises, but although he was good company it was useless to pretend she felt anything for him. And it hadn't needed Bruce to point out that he might prove to be too hot to handle.

Removing her make-up, she stared at her woebegone image in the mirror and made a face at herself. Cradle-snatching indeed! To hear Bruce Tyson talk anyone would think he was Methuselah and she a schoolgirl.

Not being on duty until midday Laurel was able to lie in the following morning. The ringing of the telephone aroused her at ten o'clock. She let it ring for a while before deciding that perhaps she ought to answer it. Sleepily she drifted downstairs, only to have the caller ring off as she reached the phone. But it was time to get up anyway so she had a leisurely breakfast and phoned home to have a chat with her father.

'And how's your friend, Dr Tyson?' he wanted to know.

'As awkward as ever.'

'Awkward? I thought him an agreeable chap. Knowledgeable too.'

'Oh, he's efficient enough, but he throws his weight around too much for my liking.'

Her father chuckled. 'You girls need keeping in order. And you don't get very far in this world by being a shrinking violet. I should have thought a strong character would have appealed to you.'

'Hmmm . . . this particular bossy-boots just gets under my skin.'

He chuckled again. 'Interesting!'

'No, just annoying. Well, I'll have to be going, Dad. Take care of yourself and I'll be down again as soon as I can.'

Her day at the hospital passed uneventfully, apart from gossip about who had been with whom at Rinaldo's party. She did not see Bruce. Moira

Carp was on leave, and so there were no hassles anywhere.

Arriving back home at ten p.m. she found more red roses waiting for her.

'Guess who?' grinned Dilys. 'Says he's rung several times today without success . . . and so he came round with these about eight. I told him you wouldn't be home till now, but he wants you to ring him. Number's on the pad.'

'Oh dear!' Laurel sighed. 'What am I going to do about this guy?'

Dilys ran her fingers through her urchin cut. 'Give him an inch and you could end up in deep water. Unless you like him, that is . . .'

'Not in that way, I don't.' Laurel chewed her lip.

'Well, ring him and put him out of his misery. I promised you would.'

Laurel picked up the phone and dialled the number. 'Paolo? This is Laurel . . .'

'*Cara mia!*' came his excited voice. 'You 'ave finished the work, huh? I come round to see you now?'

'Oh no, Paolo. I've had a hectic day. I'm going to bed. I just rang to thank you for the flowers. It's very sweet of you, but really, you shouldn't. You've done enough already.'

'So when can I see you?' he cut in. 'Tomorrow?'

'Sorry. I'm working late again.' It wasn't true, but it was the easiest way out.

'You work too 'ard. You tell me when . . . and we go for a beautiful drive somewhere, so I can 'ave you all to myself, huh?'

Laurel made a despairing face at Dilys. 'We-ell, I

won't be free until Saturday afternoon. But I expect you'll be busy then,' she added hopefully.

'Saturday afternoon? That's fine. I leave my manager to look after things and I pick you up at three?'

'Just a minute.' Laurel put her hand over the mouthpiece and appealed to Dilys in desperation. 'What can I tell him?'

'Say you're looking after next door's dog.'

'Dilys has just reminded me that I promised to look after our neighbour's labrador,' she went on. 'Y-you could come for a walk with us, in the park, if you like . . .'

There was a pause before he sighed and said, 'Okay . . . then we make a proper date for another time, huh?'

Putting the phone down, Laurel turned to Dilys looking mystified. 'When did we promise to look after the dog?'

Her friend giggled. 'We didn't. It just came to me on the spur of the moment. Mrs Wright's a good sort. She won't mind lending you Bengy if you explain. And nobody can get amorous with a sixty-pound labrador gallumphing between them.'

'Want to bet?' said Laurel gloomily. 'Well, at least it'll give me a chance to lay it on the line that there's nothing doing.'

At the first opportunity she had a word with their co-operative neighbour. The girls had on occasion looked after the dog when Mrs Wright was away for the day and now she was only too happy to loan her pet as chaperon.

Promptly at three on Saturday afternoon Paolo

appeared in his shining new dark blue Porsche. Laurel put the bouncy yellow labrador on the lead as Paolo backed away at the dog's boisterous welcome.

'This is Bengy. It's all right, he's only being friendly,' she said cheerfully. 'I usually go to Greenwich Park where he can have a good run. Is this your new car? Wow! What a beaut! Well, you certainly won't want him climbing all over it. We'll take mine, I think.'

She pulled forward the front seat of her Mini to let the dog into the back. Afterwards Paolo climbed in beside her, bunching his knees in the small space. The dog poked his wet nose between them as they drove. He sniffed curiously around Paolo's ear.

Laurel curbed a grin. 'He must like your aftershave!'

Paolo's expression was amusing, a mixture of wariness and grudging acceptance. 'I not put it on for 'im,' he said, his hand sliding onto her jeans-clad thigh.

She brushed it away, reaching for the gear lever as she slowed to turn into the park. The broad avenue of majestic chestnut trees was alight with pink and white candles of blossom, and azaleas and tulips made bold splashes of colour amid the grassy spaces. At the end of the drive Laurel parked the car near where the General Wolfe statue looked out over the vast panorama of East London.

It was a mild day of sunshine and shadow with swiftly moving white clouds in a blue sky. There were plenty of other cars parked and people out enjoying the air.

'Zis is a good place,' said Paolo, looking around at the rolling green lawns and grand old trees. 'I 'ave never been 'ere before.'

'Yes, it's very historic,' Laurel said, letting the dog off the lead.

'What is that?' He pointed to the warm-brick domed building on their right.

'That's the old Royal Observatory, you know, where Greenwich Mean Time originates?' She found a stick and threw it for the dog who chased after it enthusiastically. They repeated the performance several times until Bengy tired of the game, flopped down and decided to chew the stick instead.

''E is a sensible dog!' said Paolo approvingly. 'Now we sit also, Huh?' He stretched out on the grass, looking up at her with dark, soulful eyes. 'Come!' He patted the ground beside him.

She sat crosslegged, picked a blade of grass and twisted it, wondering how to wrap up the fact, without hurting him, that she didn't wish to continue seeing him.

He propped himself on one elbow. 'Why you look so sad, *cara mia*?'

She hesitated. 'Look, Paolo, please don't be offended, but the truth is . . . well, I did tell you I'd got a boyfriend, didn't I? So I'd rather . . . I don't think I'd better see you again.'

He sat up and moved closer, putting his arm around her shoulders and peering into her face. 'You give me the brush-off, huh? But I know it already. I feel it 'ere.' He placed a hand over his heart. 'He is a lucky guy, this boyfriend. But you give me a kiss, to show we are friends?'

She smiled in relief, glad that he had taken it so well. 'Okay,' she said.

He closed in, but it wasn't the fleeting kiss she had expected. His mouth to mouth salute was a prolonged and passionate affair which was only brought to an end by a large coloured ball hitting him on the head.

Laurel seized her chance to break away as a small boy came running up to them.

'Sorry,' he said, picking up the ball.

Her stomach lurched as she recognised the child. It was David, Bruce's son. 'Hallo, I know you, don't I? I saw you last Sunday,' she said.

He looked puzzled. 'Did you?'

'Yes, with your daddy.' Her glance went beyond him to the husky, unmistakable figure of the registrar waiting some yards off.

Paolo followed her startled gaze. He jumped up delightedly. 'It's the doctor!' he exclaimed and hurried over to shake Bruce by the hand.

Laurel sat where she was, her face burning. She knew he must have seen Paolo kissing her. Judging by his caustic remarks at the party she could well imagine what he must now be thinking.

The boy ran off towards his father and Rinaldo stayed with them to kick the ball around. The dog also decided to join in to David's delight, chasing from one to the other in pursuit of the elusive ball.

The sky had clouded over and suddenly a large spot of rain hit Laurel on the face . . . then another . . . and another. She jumped up and ran for the shelter of an old tree as the skies opened. Paolo grabbed the boy's hand, racing through the deluge towards the Pavilion with Bruce. They beckoned her to follow.

It was the last thing she wanted, a confrontation with Bruce in the company of Paolo. But at least with the child being there his attention would not be entirely concentrated on her. Calling to Bengy, she put him on the lead and with some reluctance ran to join the others.

The labrador gave himself a good shake as they all stood damp and breathless inside the doorway, wiping the rain from their faces.

'We all like some coffee, huh?' said Paolo, 'I get them.'

'No, let me.' Bruce followed him to the counter.

'Shall we sit in this corner?' Laurel said to David, 'Then Bengy will be out of the way, in case they don't like dogs in here.'

David patted the broad golden head. 'He's nice. I wish we had a dog,' he said wistfully.

'Don't you have any pets?'

'My grandma's got a cat, and we've got some hamsters at school. I'm looking after one for the holidays.'

'Well, I'm only looking after Bengy for today. He's not mine,' Laurel explained. 'Down, boy.' She pushed the dog under the table.

Perching on the edge of his chair, David propped his chin on his hands. 'My dad says we can have one when he buys a house.'

He was an attractive child with dark-fringed blue eyes just like his father. She could imagine him in early manhood being just as forthright and resolute. 'And when is he going to buy a house?' she asked curiously.

'I don't know. One day soon, he says.'

'How long have you lived with your grandma?'

'Oh, a long time. Mummy died when I was little. I don't remember her. She fell out of a boat, you know,' he said solemnly. 'She couldn't swim. I can swim, though.'

'It's good to know how to swim,' agreed Laurel.

'Can Bengy swim?'

'Well, I don't really know, David, but most dogs can. I'll tell you something though, I don't think he likes water too much. He even walks round puddles.'

They both laughed.

The two men returned with the coffee and an ice-cream for David. They were talking football and discussing the merits of their favourite teams. 'Cricket is really my game, although I don't get much chance to play these days,' Bruce said. He darted a glance at Laurel. 'How about you? Are you the sporting type?'

She sipped her coffee. 'I did athletics at school, but not since.'

'Your activities being confined to more adult games now, I suppose,' he observed drily.

Ignoring the innuendo, she gazed out of the window. 'Oh good, it looks as if the shower has eased off. I'd like to get back, if you don't mind, Paolo. I'm starting nights tonight, and I must get a couple of hours' sleep before I go on.'

'These nurses, they work too hard, no?' Paolo appealed to the doctor.

'Unsocial hours, but the job has its compensations,' Bruce said.

'Oh, I couldn't be stuck in an office from nine till five,' agreed Laurel. She finished her drink, coaxed the dog from under the table and smiled at the boy. 'Well, goodbye David. I hope you get your wish soon,' she whispered confidentially.

Paolo jumped up. 'Okay ; . . we go. *Ciao!*' He put his arm possessively around her waist as they left and made their way towards the car. 'He is a good guy, that doctor. You like 'im?'

'He's all right,' she returned carelessly.

He tapped the side of his nose with his forefinger and gave her a sly look. 'I think you like him a lot.'

Laurel grinned and unlocked the car door. 'And I think you're an incurable romantic. I don't spend my time chasing every doctor I meet.'

'They chase you, huh? Zis boyfriend, is he a doctor?'

'No, he's not.' She wound down the window to let out the smell of damp dog. 'Phew! I like dogs, but not when they're wet. Aren't you glad we came in my car?'

'I prefer to have you in my car . . . wizzout the dog.'

'Then I wouldn't have come, Paolo,' she told him. 'I did mean what I said, about not seeing you again. I'm sorry.'

He put on a rueful expression. 'This is one time I lose, huh?'

They were back at the house and she pulled up behind his Porsche. Paolo took her hand between both of his. 'So it is goodbye? I never forget you, Laurel. I kiss you one more time?'

She smiled and shook her head. 'You save your kisses for someone who appreciates them.'

He spread his arms in resignation as they stood on the pavement together. 'So I see you around sometime, maybe. You come to my restaurant and I give you dinner on the house?'

'Thank you. Maybe,' she said.

Waiting to wave him goodbye as he drove off, she watched him turn the corner before going into the next house to return Bengy to his owner.

CHAPTER SEVEN

AT SEVEN p.m. on Sunday evening, after her usual
fitful daytime efforts to sleep, Laurel rose, slipped
into her dressing-gown and trailed downstairs for
coffee before getting ready to go on night duty. She
found Emma and Dilys together in the kitchen,
tucking into tea and toast.

'Hi!' said Laurel, delighted to see the third mem-
ber of the household back with them. 'We've missed you. And you've even got a tan,' she noticed,
admiring the golden glow of Emma's fair skin.
'Been doing some sunbathing?'

'Yes . . . I went down to my married brother's at
Westgate for a couple of days. It was lovely down
there. Nice to be back though. It was a bit difficult
having to keep things to myself. Anything interesting been happening here while I've been away?'

Dilys jerked her head towards Laurel. 'She's
been fighting off her Italian admirer, Andy and I
are still pussyfooting around, and that's about it
really. Oh, and Ahmed Singh got his FRCP. Pity
you missed out on Rinaldo's party . . . it was
super.'

Laurel made her coffee, pulled up a chair and sat
down at the table to exchange gossip. Emma was
given a graphic account of the evening at Rinaldo's
and of his persistent pursuit of Laurel.

'It wasn't easy fending him off, but I took him for

a walk in the park the other day and finally managed to convince him there was nothing doing. The trouble was, he insisted on giving me a goodbye kiss. And who do you think was looking on? Tyson. I'm sure that man thinks I spend my spare time rolling in the hay with all and sundry. And me pure as the driven snow,' Laurel said indignantly.

Dilys grinned. 'I wouldn't put it quite like that. Well, now that the terrible trio is back in strength, why don't we throw a party to celebrate?'

'Oh, wait till I'm off nights, will you?' said Laurel. 'I can't rise to being sociable until I'm back to normal. We didn't even have time for a cuppa until half-three last night, but at least being busy helps you to stay awake.'

'I—I suppose Phil hasn't phoned?' Emma ventured.

The other girls shook their heads. 'Don't try and get in touch with him again, will you, Em?' said Dilys.

'Don't worry, I won't. I just wondered if you'd told him . . . if he knew . . . about me.'

'No fear,' said Laurel, 'we wouldn't give him that satisfaction.'

'Good, because that's a phase of my life I want to put behind me.' Emma gave a wan smile. 'I can't help thinking about him sometimes though. Stupid, aren't I?'

'Oh, one of these days you'll look back and wonder whatever you saw in him,' put in Dilys cheerfully. 'There'll be other blokes.'

Laurel rolled her eyes at Emma. 'She's seeing life in technicolour at the moment, just because Andy danced with her a couple of times.' Finishing her drink she stretched luxuriously and ran her fingers through her tousled locks. 'Well, I shall have to leave you two layabouts. It's back to the grindstone for me.' She went up to her room to dress.

There were four of them on duty that Sunday evening; Sister Dustin, Laurel, Mollie O'Brien and Louise, the second-year student. The department was fairly quiet and they had cleared the backlog of day cases by midnight, when an ambulance arrived bringing a middle-aged man with an acute intestinal obstruction.

His wife had followed the ambulance in her car and she gave Laurel details as the patient was wheeled along to an examination room.

'He's a barman you see, Nurse, and he's strained himself before, lifting barrels. He did this a couple of days ago and this time the lump won't go back. He's been terribly sick. He can't pass anything either.'

Mr Collins, the patient, was pale and sweaty with a rapid pulse and clearly in need of prompt attention. 'All right,' Laurel said kindly to his wife after the porters had transferred the distressed man from the trolley to the bed, 'If you'll just sit outside we'll get him ready for the doctor.'

With Louise to help, she set about the preliminaries in a calm and soothing manner. 'We'll just have your pyjamas off and pop you into a gown,' she said, 'and will you get a bottle, Louise? We'll need a urine specimen.' After recording his temperature and blood pressure, she went along to the duty doctor's bedroom just down the corridor and knocked.

'Come!' Bob Merrick answered.

She poked her head around the door. Bob had not yet retired; he was surrounded by text books, swotting for his FRCS. 'Come and get some practical experience,' Laurel said.

He patted the space beside him on the bed and gave her an impudent grin. 'How about making it worth my while?'

'Oh, shut up, Bob. There's a bloke here in a bad way.'

'Okay,' he returned good-naturedly, and bounded along beside her to see the patient.

Although he was ever ready for fun and games with any nurse who would oblige, Bob was completely businesslike when the occasion demanded. Now he carried out his examination in a brisk and competent manner, examining the purpling mass in Mr Collins' groin and sounding the distended abdomen with his stethoscope. 'No bowel sounds,' he murmured to himself. 'Mr Collins, I should think you've got a strangulated hernia here, which calls for surgery. You're very dehydrated, aren't you, with all that vomiting.' He looked across at Laurel. 'We'd better get some fluid into him, stat.'

Together they set up an intravenous glucose drip before Bob went off to put a call through to the surgical registrar.

Bruce Tyson arrived some ten minutes later. Hearing his decisive footsteps echoing along the quiet corridor, Laurel went out to meet him, her personal animosity put aside by the common bond of a job to be done. Involuntarily her heart skipped a beat at the sight of him. Woken from his sleep, he had dressed quickly in a navy blue fleecy cotton sweater and a pair of old jeans under his white coat. His thick dark hair was unbrushed and there was a shadow of growth around his chin.

'We're in here,' she said, with a half-apologetic smile, as though it were her fault he had been disturbed.

Although his rest had been interrupted, Bruce was as diligent as ever while Bob Merrick gave him a résumé of his findings. Listening to the registrar's quiet questions, watching his frowns and his smiles as he talked to the patient, Laurel experienced a stirring of emotions within her that had nothing to do with his rôle as a doctor. For all his previous truculence towards her, he had a personal magnetism which disturbed her more than she cared to admit.

'Well, Mr Collins,' Bruce said, 'there's only one way we can deal with this for you, and that is to operate. I know the theatres are fully booked for tomorrow, so I'd like to do it straight away. All right?'

'Okay, doctor, anything you say,' said Mr Collins limply.

Bruce patted his hand. 'Good man.' He turned to Laurel. 'I'll get things moving if you'll do the necessary. Pre-med Omnopon and Scopolamine.'

'Yes . . . and do you want me to pass a Ryle's tube?'

He considered for a moment. 'No, we'll do that

in theatre when he's under. It'll be easier for him that way.'

She nodded, appreciating his consideration for the patient's comfort. 'Mrs Collins is outside . . . will you tell her?'

'Right.' Bruce departed to explain matters to the anxious wife before going on to alert anaesthetist and theatre staff and to prepare himself to operate.

Bob Merrick headed for the Path Lab with a blood sample for analysis, leaving Laurel to do her part.

'It'll be good to have it over and done with tonight, won't it?' she said encouragingly to the apprehensive patient. 'Better than having all night to think about it.' She checked the drugs with Louise, drew them up and injected them. 'You'll feel a bit better when these begin to work.'

'How long will it take, Nurse?' Mr Collins asked.

'Not much more than an hour.'

He licked his dry lips. 'Oh lor, I'm a bloody coward.'

'You'll be all right, Mr Collins. You can have every confidence in Mr Tyson,' she smiled. 'He could do this job with his eyes shut . . . but I expect he'll keep them very wide open.'

He gave a feeble grin. 'Will you be coming with me?'

'I'll be taking you along to the anaesthetic room,' she said. 'Now, have you any false teeth?' He shook his head. 'Right. Shall we have your watch off? Your wife can take it home. I expect you'd like to see her for a few minutes before she goes.'

Louise made out the name tapes for attachment to the patient's wrist and ankle. Laurel listed his possessions in the Patients' Property book and put them in a plastic bag under the trolley. Then she completed the necessary paperwork while Mrs Collins sat with her husband.

'I should go home now, love,' Laurel advised when all was ready. 'There's no point in waiting around. Ring up in the morning. He'll be going to Lister Ward. And don't worry . . . he's in good hands.'

Having delivered their patient into the care of the main theatre staff, Laurel and Louise joined their colleagues in the coffee room, where Bob Merrick was also taking his ease with his feet up on a chair. After a bit of general chaffing he decided to catch up on some sleep. 'Well, goodnight folks. You know where to find me if I'm wanted.' Tweaking Laurel's hair, he ambled off again towards the doctors' bedroom.

'Would you and Louise like to take your break now?' Sister Dustin said. 'Mollie and I will go later. I've got to get down to sorting out this off-duty.' Her homely face wrinkled. 'It's the devil's own job trying to please everyone.'

Putting on their cloaks, Laurel and Louise made their way through the deserted department towards the rest room where they relaxed over egg and tomato sandwiches for half an hour, reading the current issues of popular magazines.

'I really ought to be studying,' Louise said. She had exams looming in the near future. 'Bet I don't get any of the questions I've revised. You wouldn't like to test me on the nervous system when we get back, would you?'

'Sure. Anything to keep ourselves awake,' said Laurel.

Sister Dustin and Mollie O'Brien left for their break shortly after the two girls returned. In the office they settled down to work and continued steadily for some time. Presently Laurel stifled a yawn. 'You know your stuff pretty well, Louise. I don't think you've got much to worry about. Make sure you read the questions carefully, that's the main thing. They don't give you any bonus marks for irrelevant information. And don't forget to go on about the tender loving care bit. They're hot on that.' She glanced at her watch, rubbed her sleepy eyes and stretched. 'Three a.m. I always think this is the very worst time of night. Think I'll make some more coffee.'

Going along towards the staff room, she was surprised to see Bruce approaching her from the opposite direction.

'Hallo!' he said, 'Any coffee going?'

'Yes, I'm just on my way to make some.' She wondered fleetingly why he had come back to A and E when he could easily have had a drink with Theatre Sister and the rest of the team he'd been working with.

He followed her into the staff room where he sank into an easy chair, one long leg propped across the other, hands behind his head.

She filled the kettle, plugged it in and set out three mugs. 'We should have some biscuits . . .' Stretching up, she tried to reach the tin on top of the wall cabinet, but it was too far back. The chair she climbed on wobbled alarmingly and he came to steady it, clasping his hands around her waist to help her down. His touch sent a shiver of pleasure through her and her cheeks flushed.

'You should have asked me to get that. You'll be breaking your neck. At least that might keep you out of mischief for a while,' he added wryly.

Laurel swallowed. He seemed to be in a fairly amiable mood and she wanted to keep it that way. 'I'll overlook that remark since we interrupted your beauty sleep.' She spooned instant coffee into the mugs and poured on boiling water, very conscious that his eyes followed her every movement. 'How did Mr Collins get on? Any problems?'

'All plain sailing . . . no complications.' A smile flickered at the corners of his mouth. 'You'll have to let me in on your magic formula for putting patients at ease.'

'Magic formula? Didn't know I had one.'

'It seemed to work for Mr Collins.'

'Perhaps it was your magic formula,' she said with a modest laugh. Putting his drink on the table beside him, she made for the door with a mug in her hands.

'Where are you off to now?' he demanded.

'I'm taking this to Louise.'

'Oh, well come back and talk to me. I didn't come here to sit on my own.'

She was gratified that he should have asked her. 'I was coming back,' she said, 'I shan't be a minute.' After taking the drink to the office she went back to join him, seating herself on the other side of the table. 'Didn't you go to Tonbridge this weekend?' She nibbled at a biscuit. 'I thought you'd be taking your son home.'

'Yes, I did. But he had to be back at school by six today, so I came straight on after dropping him.'

'I thought he was living with his grandparents?'

'He goes there most weekends. He's at boarding school.'

'Oh! Poor kid.'

'Why do you say that?'

Laurel lowered her eyes and concentrated on stirring her coffee. She could have kicked herself for being so tactless.

'Why did you say that?' he repeated, giving her a straight look from under his brows.

She drew a deep breath and tried to explain, wanting to keep the peace, but having to be honest. 'I wasn't meaning to be critical. It's just that, well, I think it must be tough to be living away from home when you're small. No one to fight your battles. My brother hated it. Kids can be pretty ghastly to each other. If I had children I'd opt for day school while they were young, at least.'

'You would, would you? In some circumstances the ideal isn't possible.'

'I know. I said I wasn't being critical. It was only a point of view. I suppose if you'd remarried it would have been different,' she added as an after-thought.

He grunted. 'How many women would be prepared to take on a ready-made family? In any case, I've no desire to marry again. Once was enough.'

She imagined he must still be cherishing the

memory of his dead wife. 'I'm sorry. It must have been awful for you, losing your wife like that.'

'Do I gather my past has been under discussion?'

'Not exactly. It just came up in passing when we met you at Greenwich that day. Andy mentioned there'd been a boating tragedy.'

'I see.' He paused for a moment. 'But what most of the world doesn't know is that my wife was with some other man when the accident occurred.'

Laurel was stunned into silence as the implication of his remark sank in. No wonder he had such a derisory attitude towards women if his wife had been unfaithful. 'I—I'm sorry,' she said again.

'It's a pretty boring topic,' he returned offhandedly. 'Let's talk about you. You seem to be seeing a lot of the persuasive Mr Rinaldo. What is it you like about the man?'

She gave a whimsical grin. 'Let's say he flatters my ego. He's very gallant.'

'Gallant or not, once he's pulled you he'll be off on another conquest. I know the type. Perhaps I should have been doing you a favour if I'd let him croak.' His eyes searched hers in a manner that made her hackles rise. She certainly was not going to tell him that she had come to her own conclusions on that score.

'I don't think your father would approve,' he went on.

'That's his prerogative, not yours. And he's wise enough to let me make my own decisions. I'm not a minor, you know.'

'You behave like one sometimes. Professionally

speaking you can't be faulted, but out of uniform, well . . .'

Laurel seethed. 'Thank you very much!' she snapped. 'You really can be quite objectionable when you try.' Her bleep sounding at that moment gave her the opportunity to leave him. 'Excuse me,' she said primly, and returned to the office, desperately unhappy at the way things had gone.

As she finished speaking to the Central Ambulance Centre, Sister Dustin and Mollie returned. 'There's a casualty on the way,' Laurel told them. 'A woman beaten up by a housebreaker. I'll get Bob up, shall I?'

'Yes,' said Sister, 'and did I see Tyson in the coffee room? I'd better get him to hang on in case he's needed.'

When the ambulance arrived the attendant gave them a brief summary of events. 'She was alone in her flat and she surprised this chap going through her dressing-table drawers. He laid into her . . . put the boot in. She just managed to crawl to the phone after he'd gone.'

The woman was a sorry sight. There were ugly contusions all over her face, her eyes were almost closed with swelling. Filled with compassion Sister Dustin and Laurel gently removed her torn nightdress and made their preliminary observations, noting with concern her rapid pulse and increasing pallor.

Bob Merrick's grumbles at being roused from his sleep gave way to pity and anger when he saw the state of the victim. Carefully he examined her abused body. She winced with pain when he touched the reddened swelling on her left side. 'That's bad, is it?' The woman nodded and Bob glanced meaningfully towards Bruce, who had come to lean in the doorway. 'There seems to be some rib damage, and possibly a ruptured spleen.'

The registrar came over to make his own diagnosis. He nodded in agreement. 'Yes, my dear, I think we shall have to take a look inside you.' Gently he stroked the patient's cheek with the back of his fingers. 'It may be necessary to remove your spleen, but fortunately that's something you can live without.' He smiled at her reassuringly, and aside to Bob Merrick he murmured, 'Put up a drip and get her blood cross-matched, will you?'

After writing out instructions for the X-ray department he went off to make his preparations for yet another emergency surgery session.

Laurel's tortuous feelings towards Bruce underwent an about face. She could not help appreciating the man's professionalism and the confidence he inspired. It was almost a tangible thing, the strength that passed from him to his patient. But with much to be done there was little time for self-analysis. There was the drip to set up, name-tapes to be attached, charts to be made out and X-rays to be taken. Finally, with her part in the proceedings completed and the woman safely in the hands of the theatre staff, Laurel had time for reflection.

Complex emotions ran riot through her brain as she tidied up the examination room and put clean disposable coverings on the trolley. She had tried to be indifferent to the arrogant registrar who seemed to go out of his way to antagonise her, and yet, deep-down, she knew that a kind word from Bruce, a gentle look, and she would be unable to resist him. There had been those fleeting moments when she had fancied that he might be attracted to her, until some perverse streak in both of them had destroyed the illusion.

Why did he put up this barrier of hostility between them? She cast about in her mind for a reason. Perhaps it wasn't only her. Perhaps he had a sour attitude towards all women, apart from patients, on account of his wife's infidelity? At least that threw a new light on things, since she had believed he still cherished the memory of a perfect marriage.

Laurel sighed heavily and wished she could wipe out the impression he seemed to have that she was a flirtatious butterfly. But was she in danger of falling into the old trap again? If you allowed yourself to get fond of people, you were bound to come a cropper sooner or later. Love was a dead end. It would be more sensible to steer clear of him as much as possible than to run the risk of letting her heart rule her head.

Her resolve was easy to keep for the rest of the week since Bruce was not again in the department while she was there. Nevertheless, in the small hours of the morning, when activity was at a minimum, her thoughts were constantly drawn to him and the ache in her heart became a physical pain. She wondered if she would ever get him out of her hair. At last she truly appreciated the depths of Emma's despair over Phil.

The following Saturday brought her last night on duty. Then she was due for four days' leave before going back onto days. Laurel looked forward to going home and catching up on family news. On the phone her father had told her that Tom, her brother, would be coming home from Brussels for the wedding, fixed for the second week in June. It was months since she'd seen him.

But before that there were the usual Saturday night casualties to be dealt with, and they came in thick and fast. A drunk, an attempted suicide, a fractured femur and a motor-cyclist with multiple injuries.

It was eleven-thirty when the police brought in a man with his face razor-slashed during a gang vendetta. Moira Carp was duty casualty officer. She had kept Bruce talking after consulting him about the motor-cyclist, and she was none too pleased at having their tête-à-tête cut short.

In the minor ops theatre Laurel waited to assist her with stitching the slashed face. Standing on the far side of the table, Moira was in a foul mood as she smoothed on her sterile gloves. Opposite her, Laurel began stripping the covering off the suturing pack.

'Come along, Nurse,' said Moira tetchily, 'You should have everything ready by now.'

Laurel ignored the unjust outburst. She handed Moira the hypodermic and was about to break open the ampoule of Lignocaine when the sound of rushing feet in the corridor made her pause. Moira's startled glance went past her to where the door burst open. Laurel turned around to look. She saw a long-haired lout in a metal-studded leather jacket, bulging eyes darting towards the patient on the bed. There was a glint of steel in his fist.

'I'm gonna get you, mate!' he hollered, drew back his arm and threw the knife.

Moira screamed. The patient put up an arm to shield himself. Spontaneously Laurel moved to protect him . . . The knife struck her in the neck, just above the collar-bone.

She put up her hand to it in disbelief. Apart from the initial sharp impact she felt no pain. With the weight of the handle the knife fell to the grey-tiled floor. Her blood gushed forth. Bright red arterial blood, pumping out all over her white uniform, staining the wall opposite, the bed, pooling on the floor. It all seemed unreal.

Moira was screaming hysterically, yelling for help. Laurel wanted to tell her to calm down, but the words would not come. Her head began to spin and her legs to sag. She was vaguely aware of struggling figures in the doorway. She thought she heard Bruce's voice from a long way off. Then she pitched forward. Her head struck a corner of the oxygen stand, and she knew no more.

She did not see the agony in the registrar's eyes as he rushed to staunch the flow of blood, or the anxiety of Sister Dustin and her sharp rebuke to the uncontrolled Moira Carp, or the fury of the porters as they marched the ruffian away to await the police. She was unaware of the frantic haste with which they rushed her to the resuscitation room.

CHAPTER EIGHT

LAUREL had the most awful headache. For ages she seemed to have been struggling in vain to reach a dim light in a fog of darkness. The deep voice which penetrated the cottonwool dulling her brain reached her from a distance.

'Squeeze my hand, Laurel, if you can hear me.'

She was aware of a hand holding hers, strong and comforting. She tried to open her eyes to see who was there but her lids were too heavy; her whole body felt like a dead weight. Her mouth was dry and her temples throbbed. She wanted to put a hand to her forehead, but it seemed to be pinned down somehow.

The voice was nearer now, and insistent. 'Squeeze my hand, Laurel.' It brooked no refusal and, weakly, she returned the pressure.

'Good!' the voice encouraged, 'Now open your eyes and look at me.'

Making a tremendous effort she lifted her lids. At first everything was fuzzy, but gradually objects swam into view. The thing anchoring her right forearm was a splint which held in place the canula attached to a drip-feed. There was a pale green counterpane on the cot-sided bed she was in. Her eyes travelled upwards from the large hand which still grasped hers, coming to focus on the tense face of the registrar. Emma was there too, in uniform beside him, looking down at her anxiously.

Laurel blinked and passed a tongue over her dry lips. She tried to collect her thoughts. What was she doing there, presumably on Emma's ward? She attempted to sit up, but the effort was too much and her head fell back against the flat pillow. There was a dull ache somewhere in the region of her right shoulder. A gleam of light danced off the metal of the stethoscope around Bruce's neck. It brought a flash of memory . . . a memory of a steel blade streaking towards her . . . and all that pulsing blood. She must have passed out.

'Did I faint?' she asked feebly.

Bruce's taut expression relaxed and his mouth twitched. 'Something like that.'

'What's the time?'

'High time you woke up, young lady. It's lunch-time, and it's Tuesday.'

'Tuesday?' she repeated, frowning.

He still held her hand tightly as though to prevent her from slipping away from them again. 'Yes, you've been out for almost two days.'

'Oh!' She felt very stupid for being such a liability. 'Sorry.'

He released her hand. 'Can you feel your fingers?'

She moved them cautiously and wondered why he asked. 'Yes . . . they're all right.'

'No tingling?'

'No.'

Bruce glanced towards Emma. 'The nerve's okay.'

'Why am I on Neuro?' puzzled Laurel.

Emma smiled. 'You knocked yourself out when you fell.'

'There's no fracture, but you've been concussed. I'd better take a look at her neck,' Bruce said to Emma.

She pulled apart the velcro shoulder-fastening of the hospital gown which Laurel was wearing, lifting back the dressing to reveal the three-inch cut at the base of Laurel's neck.

'Yes, that's looking fine. The knife nicked your carotid,' he explained, replacing the dressing. 'You should have ducked instead of putting yourself in the line of fire, you silly child. How does the head feel?'

'Pretty ghastly.'

He laid a hand on her forehead, smoothing back the brown curls and examining the swollen graze in her hairline. 'I'm not surprised. You can't go bouncing your cranium on cast-iron with no after-effects.'

There was something remarkably like tenderness in his eyes. She had a ridiculous desire to be gathered into his arms and held against his broad chest.

She let out a long breath. 'May I have a drink?'

Emma refastened the hospital gown. 'Just a little, you don't want to be sick.' She filled a feeding cup from the jug on the locker and held it to her friend's lips. The cool water, trickling down Laurel's parched throat, tasted like nectar.

'You can dispense with the drip as soon as it runs out,' Bruce told Emma. He went to the bottom of the bed, picked up the chart hanging there and wrote instructions. 'I'm giving her some Paramol for the headache.' He smiled at Laurel. 'You'll soon be feeling better. The police want to interview you, but we'll keep them at bay for a while.' Still smiling, he went away.

Laurel's eyes followed him, bemused. 'He's being nice to me!'

Emma fussed with the pillow and bedclothes. 'Of course he is. You had a close shave, Laurel. You've had us all worried sick.'

'He smiled at me,' muttered Laurel, half to herself.

'Well, don't sound so surprised,' chuckled Emma, 'the things you've been babbling on about in your paralytic state were enough to make a cat laugh.'

'What did I say?'

'Oh, mostly unintelligible . . . you know the daft things people say when they're semi-conscious.' Emma changed the subject. 'I'll bring you in a respectable nightie now that you're back in the land of the living, and I'll get you another pillow presently. You father has come, by the way. He's been talking to Bruce, but he went off to lunch with one of the consultants just before you surfaced. He'll be back soon I expect.'

Laurel closed her eyes and passed a hand over her aching brow.

'Feeling rotten, are you?' said Emma sympathetically. 'Don't try to talk any more . . . I'll get you those tablets.'

Waiting for the sedative to take effect, Laurel lay in a drowsy faraway state before dropping off to sleep. She pondered absently on the miracle of Bruce being nice to her. But then, I'm a patient now, she reminded herself. And Bruce was always nice to his patients.

She awoke a couple of hours later, still with a headache but it wasn't quite so severe. Dr Swann was by her bedside, passing the time reading a paper. He kissed her pale cheek. 'Hallo, my darling. You mustn't go giving me shocks like this, you know. Bad for my ulcer.'

She responded with a weary smile. 'Sorry about that, Dad. You needn't have worried. I'm tough.'

'Tough or not, you can't go severing arteries willy-nilly. Lucky for you, expert help was on the spot. You should get danger money working in A and E,' he remarked drily. 'Or perhaps a course in the art of self-defence wouldn't be a bad thing. Well, how do you feel now?'

'A bit better . . . I could do with a cuppa.'

'That's a good sign. I'll have a word with your friend.'

He went away to find Emma and she came in presently with tea and biscuits for them both. She stayed to talk for a while. 'Dilys went home during her lunch hour and picked up your nightie, so we'll make you look decent in a minute. There's bound to be a run of visitors once word gets around that you've come to at last.'

'I've been talking to Tyson,' Laurel's father said. 'He thinks you should be fit for discharge by the end of the week. You'll come home then, of course. Ingrid and I had considered putting off the wedding, but perhaps now there'll be no need. In a couple of weeks you'll be as good as new,' he beamed.

'Well, if you'll excuse me, I'd better get back to the ward.' Emma gathered up the tea things. 'I'll be bringing you some supper later.' She left them happily discussing family matters.

'I phoned Tom. He said should he come over, but there didn't seem to be any point while you weren't conscious. He'll be anxious to know how you are.'

Laurel was pleased to think her brother had been ready to drop everything to visit her. 'Oh, tell him not to bother coming,' she said. 'I'll see him at the wedding, won't I?'

'Yes, he'll be over a couple of days beforehand, so we can have a family reunion then. I shall ring him this evening to let him know all's well.'

She smothered a yawn. 'You must be tired, kitten,' said Dr Swann. He glanced at his watch, 'and I ought to be getting back. I've a business meeting in the morning. Would you like me to come again?'

'Don't trouble, Dad. I shan't be neglected and as you say, I'll probably be home at the weekend.'

'Well, if you're quite sure. We'll arrange about transport for you when the time comes. God bless, darling.' He kissed her goodbye and she let her eyes close again, feeling spent with the effort of talking.

When Bruce called in on her at nine o'clock that evening she had been washed and put into her own pretty nightdress, her hair was combed and the drip apparatus removed from her arm. She had also managed a lightly scrambled egg and she felt a great deal better, although her head still swam when she tried to sit up.

'Hallo . . . and how are you tonight?' he asked, striding into her sideward and wrapping his strong hand around her wrist. 'What's all the commotion going on in here?' There was a mischievous gleam at the back of his searching gaze.

She had felt her pulse accelerate as he approached and she was suddenly shy, wondering what she had revealed in her ramblings. 'You tell me . . . you're the doctor,' she murmured, with a hint of her old spirit.

'My goodness, we are feeling better. In fighting form again, I'm glad to see.'

She stole a glance at him from under her curling lashes, and they exchanged grins. He was *still* being nice to her despite that familiar air of patronage. She found herself wishing she could go on being a patient, not getting well too quickly, so that he would have to keep coming to see her. Tears pricked the back of her eyes. She bit her lips to stop them trembling. Surprisingly gentle, he stroked her cheek in the manner she had seen him adopt with other vulnerable patients. 'Take it easy,' he said in a soft voice. 'You'll feel better after a goodnight's sleep.'

When he had gone she indulged in a little cry but had pulled herself together by the time the night staff came to settle her down.

There was no lack of visitors for Laurel over the next few days. The chief nursing officer came to see her and practically all the staff from A and E called in at odd moments. Her room became a kind of pop-in parlour, and the place began to fill with flowers, which included two lovely bouquets from Ingrid and her brother.

The police sergeant Bruce had mentioned also came to ask if she would care to make a statement. 'Glad you're better, miss. I tried to see you earlier, but they said you weren't up to it.' He sat down beside her, notebook at the ready. 'Would you like to give me your version of what happened?'

'Well, there's not much I can tell you really, except that this guy burst into the theatre where we were working and threw a knife. I expect the others saw most of the action. I didn't even get a proper look at him before I passed out.'

'Ah!' He scratched his cheek with the end of his ballpoint. 'Do you want to prefer charges?'

'Oh, no,' said Laurel. 'He didn't mean to hurt me. I just got in the way.'

The sergeant smiled. 'That's a charitable way of putting it. Most people wouldn't see it like that. It's entirely up to you of course. We've already got a string of charges against the fellow. He was high on drugs for a start.'

Laurel looked pensive. 'Poor chap . . . one of life's misfits. I won't add to his problems. All I want is to forget all about it.'

'Okay, miss. It's your decision.' The sergeant put his notebook away and shook her by the hand. 'Good luck, love. Can't afford to have our nurses put out of action, can we?'

She was sitting out in a chair when Bruce next came to see her. 'Well, how does it feel to be vertical again?' He pushed back her hair to look at the healing scar on her forehead.

'Great,' she said.

He drew the floral curtains to screen her bed from the corridor. 'Slip off your dressing gown . . . I'd better take a look at you.'

She had been hoping he wouldn't ask, but there was no help for it. Her nightdress was sleeveless and sheer, surely the beat of her heart must be clearly visible beneath the thin silk. She felt almost naked as he inspected her injury. And he had probably seen a great deal more of her than that, she realised, a flush creeping over her cheeks.

'We can have those stitches out in a couple of days,' he pronounced in a matter-of-fact voice. He helped her into her gown again. 'Then I suppose you'll be wanting to go home?'

She retied the belt around her waist. 'Yes. I—I haven't thanked you for looking after me.'

He stroked his long straight nose and regarded her keenly. 'I'm beginning to think what you need is a permanent bodyguard. We'd better keep you in over the weekend. Don't want to risk any relapse after your concussion. And how are you going to get home? You're not to drive yourself.'

'Dilys has offered to take me.'

'Hmm . . . I'm going your way on Tuesday. I'd better take you myself.' He was gone before she had a chance to argue.

Laurel let out a long breath of exasperation. There he goes again, she thought, making decisions for me without so much as a by-your-leave. She should have told him to get lost. And yet the prospect of being in his company for an hour now that he was being more agreeable had its attractions. But it was usually at weekends that he visited Tonbridge. Why was he going mid-week? she wondered.

Her wound healed well, and with no side effects from her concussion, Laurel made a good recovery. On Monday afternoon Dilys drove her back to the house where the friends spent a quiet evening together while Laurel packed for her journey home.

'Well, you can't say it's boring being at the Riversdale,' said Dilys, 'and at least this has got Moira Carp off your back. She's gone. Decided to have a nervous breakdown, so Andy says, after your knife-throwing episode.'

'Really?' said Laurel. 'Who's taking her place?'

'They've got a locum in pro tem . . . chap named Benders. I don't know much about him.'

'Anyone must be an improvement on Moira.' Laurel flipped through some of the clothes in her wardrobe. 'I'm going to have to get something new for this wedding. Better wait until I know what colour Ingrid is wearing, I suppose.'

Emma looked at her watch. 'Come on, time you were in bed.'

'I've got to wash my hair first. It's a mess.'

'Okay, if you must,' said Dilys, 'but get a move on.'

Laurel grinned. 'Will you two stop behaving like a pair of maiden aunts?'

'Well, we promised His Lordship we'd keep our

eyes on you,' Dilys told her. 'He seems to be taking an extraordinary interest in your welfare.'

'Probably because he and my father have been getting their heads together,' said Laurel. 'Men!'

Emma and Dilys had both left for work when Bruce arrived to collect Laurel the following morning. He shepherded her to the car and saw her comfortably seated before putting her luggage into the boot. He was looking particularly elegant in a well-tailored grey chalk-striped suit with a pale blue shirt and college tie.

'You're dressed to kill,' she remarked lightly as they set off. 'Are you going to some high-powered conference?'

'A business meeting actually. I'll probably be leaving the Riversdale fairly soon—going into general practice.'

She darted a glance at him, a chill of disappointment creeping over her. He was planning to leave? She might never see him again! 'Oh!' she said, and turned her eyes to the winding road ahead, not seeing anything. What a fool she was even to allow herself to think about him in any other way than as a colleague. She should have heeded her own advice to steer clear of emotional attachments. If you loved you laid yourself wide open to heartache.

Bruce gave her a sideways look. 'Just "oh"? I thought you'd be full of questions. You're not usually so monosyllabic.'

She tried to keep her voice steady. 'Well, I suppose it's the logical step. I hope it works out for you.'

'Thank you. I hope to have it all tied up by the

time you're back in circulation.' A smile flickered at the corners of his mouth. 'And by that time, I gather, the wedding of the year will be over and you will have a stepmother?'

'Yes,' she said. 'I don't suppose things will ever be quite the same at home again, but I have to accept that. My father needs someone.'

'Change is the name of the game, Laurel. Nothing stays the same for ever.'

'No.' She couldn't trust herself to say more. She didn't relish change. Familiar things were more comfortable. When she'd first started nursing it had been a wrench to leave home. When she had finished her training she had hated leaving the Royal Heathside. She would be sad to leave the Riversdale and Emma and Dilys when the time came to move on, which was bound to happen sooner or later. Bruce was right. Nothing stayed the same for ever, and his leaving would start the disintegration of her world all over again.

'That was a heavy sigh,' he said.

She affected a careless laugh. 'Was it? I suppose I shall be glad when the wedding is over and it's all gone off without a hitch. Not that it's going to be a big affair,' she chatted on with forced gaiety, 'but there's always a lot to think about, ends to tie up.'

'And will young Lothario be there?'

'You mean Gary? I don't know. Probably. He's like one of the family. I know one person who'll be pleased when you become a GP,' she went on. 'David told me you'd promised him a dog when you bought a house of your own.'

'He's been confiding in you, has he? That's one

of the reasons why I decided to make the change, so that I can make a home for him.'

'Then I hope your plans work out for his sake. He's a nice kid.'

Bruce raised his eyebrows. 'It seems to be a mutual admiration society.'

They talked of less important things until arriving at her home at midday. He carried her suitcase to the door but declined to go in. 'I mustn't be late for my appointment. I shall pick you up on Sunday week to take you back,' he told her. 'Enjoy yourself, but mind you don't overdo it.'

With a feeling of despondency she watched him drive away before putting her key in the lock and going into the house. Mrs Jones came into the hall to greet her. 'There you are, my love.' They kissed fondly. 'The doctor had to go out, but he'll be back later.' Her kind face creased with concern. 'How are you feeling? Would you like to go to bed? I can bring some lunch up to your room . . .'

Laurel laughed. 'Good heavens, no. I'm not an invalid, Jonesy. I'm better.'

'Well, it was a nasty business by what your father said. Touch and go for a while.' She shook her head. 'It's a blessing we can't see what's before us, isn't it?'

In the large homely kitchen that had seen so many family breakfasts, Mrs Jones made coffee and delighted in fussing over her erstwhile charge. 'Now show me what that ruffian did to you.'

Untying the neck of her frilled blouse, Laurel showed the red scar at the base of her neck. The housekeeper tutted and stroked it with a gentle finger. 'You'd think at least you'd be safe in a hospital. Young thugs . . . I don't know what the country's coming to. I suppose you'll be able to tone that down with a bit of make-up?'

'Yes . . . and it will fade in time.' Laurel retied her blouse. 'It won't show too much and I can wear high necks for a bit. Good job frills are fashionable.'

They stayed talking for a while and then the housekeeper carried Laurel's case upstairs for her and left her to unpack. 'I'll get a light lunch presently, and there'll be a proper meal this evening, when your father gets back.'

It was good to be back in her old room with the trappings of childhood about her. There was the china piggy-bank on the windowsill . . . Tom had given her that for a birthday present. The lavender Doulton lady had belonged to her grandmother. On the wall was the little cuckoo clock she had bought on a school holiday to Austria, it had never gone properly but it was pretty with its surround of carved wooden ivy leaves. The framed watercolour of irises had been a gift from her mother.

She opened the wardrobe to put away some of her clothes and her old school satchel fell out from the bottom. Stretching full length on the bed, Laurel leafed through some of her old exercise books, recalling the faces of masters and mistresses as she read their scribbled corrections and comments. It all seemed centuries ago. So much had happened since then. She was a completely different person now.

'Change is the name of the game,' she murmured

to herself, unconsciously repeating Bruce's words. It brought him back to the forefront of her mind. She wondered how his meeting was going, which only served to underline the fact that soon he would be passing out of her life for ever.

With a lump choking her throat, Laurel buried her face in her pillow and wept. At length she blew her nose and berated herself soundly for being an idiot. Self-pity got you nothing but red eyes. Bruce Tyson could go to hell for all she cared. She had her career. Romance was just a pain in the neck. She went to the bathroom, bathed her eyes and powdered her nose before joining Mrs Jones for lunch.

Dr Swann returned around six that evening, by which time Laurel had resolved to come to terms with reality and put on a cheerful face.

'Pour me a drink, darling,' he said, relaxing in his favourite chair in the sitting-room.

'Only a small one, Dad, it's not too good for your tum.'

'You're as bad as Ingrid. What with her, and you, and Mrs Jones, I can see I'm in danger of becoming henpecked.'

'I'll believe that when it happens!' retorted Laurel. She looked around at the faded green velvet curtains and the once fresh-patterned wallpaper. 'This room needs a face-lift.'

'Yes, it does, doesn't it? But Ingrid will smarten us up a bit once we're married.' He loosened his tie and stretched in contentment. He was in the best of spirits and not looking at all tired.

'Have you been working, Dad? I thought you

were not going to start again until after your honey-moon?'

He peered at her over the rim of his glass. 'I haven't been seeing patients. Richard and I were interviewing an applicant for our new junior part-ner. You remember I said we were going to take on another man.'

'Was he any good?'

'Oh yes, he'll do fine.' Her father's eyes twink-led. 'I had no doubt about that from my first meeting with him, but of course Richard had to be convinced as well. You know him, by the way.'

Laurel looked askance. 'I do? Who is it?'

He took a sip of his drink. 'Your friend Bruce Tyson.'

She caught her breath. 'Good God!'

'Is that all you can say? I thought you might be rather pleased.'

'I—I . . . He never mentioned anything about it this morning.'

'Perhaps he preferred to wait until it was a fait accompli. He has another six weeks to do at the Riversdale, which will suit us nicely. Yes, I'm sure we've found the right man. He plans to buy a house in the area, but until then he says he can easily commute from his parents' home.'

'Oh!' said Laurel. 'That will be nice for his little boy.' She wondered how he would manage. She supposed he would get a housekeeper.

'Yes . . . apparently he has marriage plans,' Dr Swann said casually.

Bruce had marriage plans? The news struck her like a blow in the chest. Gone were her resolutions to forget the man. She had to acknowledge the fact that while he was still free she had been clinging on to the possibility that they might not lose touch. Now she was forced to admit the true depths of her feelings for him. Misery wrapped around her like a cloak.

'Ingrid will be over after dinner this evening,' her father was saying. 'She's done nothing about wedding clothes yet. She's hoping you'll go shopping with her if you feel up to it.'

'Yes, of course.' Laurel made herself sound enthusiastic. 'I'll need to get something for myself, too. Mustn't let the side down, must I?' She sat on the arm of his chair and planted a kiss on his head.

'I'm glad you're happy about things,' he said with a satisfied air.

Happy about things? She wondered if she would ever be truly happy again. Undoubtedly Ingrid meant to go out of her way to make her welcome, but even so, with Bruce being the new partner, he too might be a frequent visitor at the house. How could she bear the prospect of bumping into him and his new wife under her father's roof? It seemed as if even her own home was likely to become a no-go area for her in the near future.

CHAPTER NINE

'You are sure you feel equal to a day in town with me, Laurel?' Ingrid queried later that evening. They had been discussing colours and flowers and reception arrangements and guests for the wedding. 'Only, I don't mind if you . . .'

'Of course I'm up to it,' Laurel assured her enthusiastically, 'I'm really looking forward to it. I haven't been to the West End on a shopping spree for ages.' She was determined to do all she could to be as helpful as possible. 'Let's go soon, shall we? There's not all that much time. When can you make it?'

Ingrid said she would be free on Tuesday. Accordingly they met early that day at the station, taking the train to Charing Cross and thence on to Knightsbridge. After trying on a number of garments in the model department of one of the smart fashion stores, Ingrid decided on a turquoise silk two-piece.

'Oh, that's gorgeous,' Laurel said, standing back to admire it. 'And no alterations necessary. Dad will fall for you all over again in that.'

Having settled on Ingrid's dress, they looked for something for Laurel. She chose a cinnamon linen suit and a ruffled cream silk blouse. She was to be a witness at the register office ceremony, and her choice of colour would harmonise well with Ingrid's.

A visit to the millinery department followed, where Ingrid teamed her outfit with a matching wide-brimmed straw hat and Laurel found a jaunty piece of nonsense with a curling feather.

Pleased with their purchases, they paused for lunch at a restaurant in the store and lingered, talking over coffee.

'You'll have to observe all the traditions,' Laurel said. 'Old and new, that's easy, and your dress is blue. Now, something borrowed . . . what can I lend you?'

Ingrid laughed. 'I don't know. I've really got all I need.'

Laurel thought for a moment, then fingered the gold chain around her neck. It had been a present for her twenty-first birthday. 'I know you've got one of your own, but would you like to wear this?'

'Yes, if you'd like me to. Thank you,' Ingrid smiled. 'My parents will be arriving from Stockholm on Thursday week,' she went on. 'I've booked them in at the Splendide Hotel, and when your brother Tom gets here Alex thought it would be nice for us all to dine there, so that we can meet each other beforehand.'

'That's great. I was thinking we ought to arrange something of the sort. And what is happening about our Mrs Jones? Will she be staying on with you and Dad?'

'But of course. We couldn't do without her yet. I'll still be keeping my job as matron of the nursing home for the time being. I don't want to give up work entirely, although I shall do when Alex retires. He wants us to travel. Your friend is to be the new partner, I hear?'

'It seems so,' said Laurel non-commitally.

'How do you like the idea?'

'It doesn't affect me one way or the other. He'll do a good job for them. He's very thorough.'

Finishing their meal, they went on to complete their shopping, buying shoes and cosmetics before returning home. Having spent a day in each other's company they had come to know one another a great deal better. Ingrid was a warm-hearted person with a generous spirit. Laurel felt sure that things were going to work out well for her father.

Tom brought his car over on the hovercraft, driving down from Ramsgate and arriving at eleven p.m. on the Thursday before the wedding.

'Tom!' Laurel squealed with delight when she let him in.

'Hi, kid!' Brother and sister hugged each other.

He was a slighter edition of their father, with the same fresh complexion and twinkling hazel eyes. Laurel stood back and tugged at the neat dark beard which outlined his chin. 'How long have you been sporting this?'

'A few months. Improves my manly charm, don't you think?'

She made a face at him. 'You're putting on weight!'

'Just getting into my prime, you mean.'

'Who are you kidding? Too much living it up,' she teased. 'Are you still foot-loose and fancy free?'

'Give or take a few birds. I'm not about to compete with Dad in the matrimonial stakes though. How about you? When are you walking Gary down the aisle?'

'I'm not. We've split.'

'I didn't know.' Her brother raised a wary eyebrow. 'Are you shattered?'

'No, glad actually.'

'That's okay then. I never thought he was quite right for you somehow. I'm being transferred to our San Francisco branch in a couple of months. Since you're free, when I get settled out there you must come and spend a holiday with me.'

'San Francisco? Oh, Tom, we'll see even less of each other then.' Her eyes misted over. Absolutely everything seemed to be in the melting pot. But she took a grip on herself. For the time being, at least, they were here all together, and she had better make the most of it.

Dr Swann came down from the bathroom in his dressing gown and placed an arm affectionately round his son's shoulders. 'Hallo, my boy! So glad you could come.'

Tom grinned. 'I wasn't going to miss out on the bubbly, was I? Why don't we have a practice run now, eh?'

'You can have a lager,' said Laurel, 'but father's got to go easy on the booze if he's any consideration for his ulcer. I'll make you a milk drink, Dad. Would you like something to eat, Tom?'

'Can you find me a sandwich?'

She left them to chat while she went to the kitchen to see to their needs.

Mrs Jones had been out visiting her daughter. She arrived back as Laurel carried the tray into the living-room. It was like old times as they sat yarning about things past and present, catching up on each others' news.

'Who've we got coming on Saturday?' Tom wanted to know.

'There's your Uncle Julius and Mary, Richard Grantham and his wife, of course. Ingrid's folks and a few close friends . . . we shall be thirty in all.' Dr Swann went on to speak of their pre-wedding plans for dinner with Ingrid's parents. 'You'll like them, they're a nice couple, the Spelens. I've met them once before.'

The get-together the following evening proved to be a happy start to the main event. Both Mr and Mrs Spelen spoke English and were obviously approving of their daughter's fiancé. Sitting next to Laurel, Mr Spelen confided, 'We did not ourselves get married until late in life, which is why we have only the one child. Now Ingrid will have a brother and sister. That is nice.'

Laurel smiled at him. 'Yes, it's nice for us, too. We couldn't be more pleased.'

The wedding day dawned fine and warm. Laurel felt proud as she and Tom accompanied their father to the register office. He looked so distinguished, she thought, in his grey morning suit and topper.

'I'm as nervous as a boy,' he confessed, while

they waited in the ante-room with some of the guests.

Brushing a stray hair from his shoulders, Laurel laughed. 'You? It's only girls who are supposed to get the vapours.'

Ingrid arrived, looking svelte and beautiful, wearing a corsage of dainty orchids on her jacket. They made a handsome couple as they went into the registrar's hall to tie the bond.

Watching her father slide the ring on to Ingrid's finger, a look of tenderness in his eyes, Laurel gulped. It was a kind of revelation to discover that age was no barrier to ecstasy. Surreptitiously she reached for her handkerchief and wiped away a tear. Tom squeezed her hand. She could not help thinking of her mother. But it was no use dwelling on the past. Life had to go on. You had to adjust to changing circumstances. And Ingrid was going to be good for her father, she was sure.

After the ceremony friends and relatives crowded round to kiss the bride and offer congratulations. They all posed for photographs in the garden of the civic buildings before setting off in their cars for the reception in a nearby country hotel.

To Laurel's relief Gary was not among the guests. He was on holiday abroad, so his parents told her when she politely enquired after him.

With speeches, toasts, and the reading of telegrams the celebrations came to an end. Ingrid and Dr Swann said their goodbyes and left for a honeymoon in the Bahamas amid a flurry of rice and confetti.

Once the bride and groom had gone, it wasn't long before the rest of the party began to drift away.

'You must come and see us in Stockholm,' Mrs Spelen said warmly to Laurel as she and her husband prepared to return to their hotel to pack for their journey home.

'Thank you,' Laurel smiled. 'Maybe I'll take you up on that one of these days.' They exchanged kisses and she wished them a safe journey home.

Saying goodbye to the last of their guests, Tom went to settle the account while Laurel gathered up the wedding gifts that had arrived and collected the remainder of the wedding cake. They then drove home with Mrs Jones and the three of them spent a nostalgic evening, all feeling a little flat now that the festivities were over.

The housekeeper had come to them as a young widow when her own daughter was twelve and Laurel a toddler. She had been a good friend to the family.

'Do you think you're going to get on all right with Ingrid?' Laurel asked.

'Oh yes, love. We shall get on well enough, and she'll be working most days. Of course, she's bound to want to make changes, and you can't blame her. But I'll be retiring myself before long. My son-in-law is going to build me a granny-flat alongside their house. He's in the building trade, you know.'

Stretched out in his father's chair Tom lit up a cigar and exhaled a stream of aromatic smoke. 'Good for you, Jonesy.' He looked at his sister.

'What are your plans, kid? Anything lined up?'

She shook her head. 'You know me . . . I just wait for things to happen.'

He wagged a finger at her. 'Uh-uh! You have to go out there and *make* things happen . . . or life passes you by.'

'It's all very well for you,' retorted Laurel with a rueful grin. 'It's still very much a man's world.'

Mrs Jones smiled wisely. 'Don't you believe it. They might think they rule the roost, but we know better.'

'Jonesy!' said Tom severely, 'That's heresy. I shan't send you any more birthday cards.'

She laughed. 'So long as you don't forget to send me an invite to your wedding, when you can find someone to put up with you. Well, I'll be off to my bed, dears, goodnight.'

Tom poured more drinks for Laurel and himself and they talked into the small hours.

'I'll have to be away early in the morning to catch the hovercraft,' Tom said when they had covered every aspect of their separate lives. 'Don't you bother to get up to see me off. I'll probably be back again before I go to San Fran, so see you then. G'night, kid.' They embraced each other and parted.

It was ten-thirty the following morning when Mrs Jones popped her head into Laurel's room. 'Dr Tyson on the phone for you.'

Laurel slipped out of bed and took the call on the extension in her father's bedroom. 'Hallo?'

'Sorry if I woke you,' Bruce's deep voice sounded in her ear.

'Oh, that's okay. I was awake, I was only lying there thinking about things.'

'Was it a successful day?'

'Terrific. No hitches. One feels a bit deflated when it's all over, though.'

'I imagine so. But then, you can't be on a high all the time.'

He sounded on top of the world, and he had every reason to be, she supposed, remembering that his plans had gone well.

'I'll pick you up around six,' he went on. 'We can have a meal together somewhere on the way back.'

'Okay, thanks. That'll be fine.'

He still had said nothing about the interview with her father and Dr Grantham, although surely he must have known that it would have been discussed. Well, if that was the way he wanted to play it, she could keep her own counsel too.

Sorting out things in her room, packing to go back, she got quite incensed thinking about him. 'Damned hypocrite,' she muttered, slamming drawers and flinging things into her case. All that bull about 'once was enough' and here he was planning to get married again, if her father were correct.

She wondered about the girl in question. Was it Moira, or someone not connected with the Riversdale? Perhaps it was someone he knew at Tonbridge. Well, she would show him that it was immaterial to her what he did. She would be charmingly unconcerned, and maybe she could dent that impenetrable armour of his. He was only a man after all, probably as susceptible to a few feminine wiles as the next man. And there was quite a bit of truth in what Mrs Jones had said.

Laurel dressed with care that evening. She decided to wear her wedding outfit. The frilly blouse was flattering and she knew she looked good.

Bruce's eyes expressed approval when he saw her, but he passed no comment. 'I know of a good place where we can eat,' he said, turning the car away from London. 'I booked for seven, so we've plenty of time.' He pulled into the spacious grounds of a country club set well back from the road. 'Pleasant, isn't it? Shall we sit here and talk for a bit?'

The evening was warm and a blackbird trilled its evensong. A climbing yellow rose sprawled in profusion over the entrance to the building and there was a border of multi-coloured irises in full bloom.

'Yes, it's quite idyllic,' she agreed, leaning back in her seat, the creamy silk of her blouse nestling against her throat.

'You look like a piece of fragile porcelain,' he remarked, his eyes assessing her.

'Appearances can be deceptive. I can assure you I'm not at all fragile.'

There was a moment of silence before he said, 'I take it you know?'

He was wearing such a self-satisfied expression she could have hit him. 'Know what?' she asked, her eyes wide with assumed innocence.

'That I'm to join your father's practice.'

'Oh, *that*. Yes, I know all about that.'

'Well?'

Laurel gave a short laugh. 'It's no concern of

mine, Bruce. I'm glad for your son's sake though.' Her guard slipped a little as she thought of the eager-faced young boy. 'You'll be able to see more of each other. It's what you were both wanting, isn't it?'

'Yes.' He paused and leaned towards her, resting one arm on the wheel, looking into her face. 'And now that I'm to become one of the family, so to speak, does that entitle me to privileged treatment?'

She looked puzzled. 'What privileged treatment?'

'You once told me that Gary Grantham was like one of the family, which was why he was entitled to take liberties with you.'

Panic gripped her and and her cheeks burned. She drew a tremulous breath and said in a low voice. 'You did that once before without being privileged, if I remember.'

'At Rinaldo's party, you mean?'

She dropped her gaze and studied her nails.

'I apologise for that. Maybe I misread the situation. Can't we be friends?'

'Why not?' she returned sweetly, glancing up at him from under her thick lashes. 'It's much more agreeable.'

Her heart bounded as he moved purposefully towards her. Taking her chin in his hand, he regarded her with a quizzical smile before deliberately putting his lips to hers. She offered no resistance, neither did she allow herself to respond. Then his hand stroked the back of her neck as he drew her closer. His fingers reaching up into her hair made her long to give herself without reserve, to return his kiss with all the longing she felt. She had resolved to be cool and controlled, but it took all her will-power not to relax in his arms.

Deliberately she pushed him away and smoothed her hair. 'Privilege has its limits,' she said carelessly, as though being kissed long and ardently by male escorts left her unmoved. 'My father did mention that you had plans to marry again.'

He sat back, his deep blue eyes unwavering, a half-smile curving the corners of his mouth. 'That's right.'

'And what would your prospective partner think if she could have seen you making a pass at me?' Her own eyes flashed angrily as she returned his frank gaze.

Not the least disconcerted, he appeared to find the situation amusing. 'I think she might approve.'

Laurel tossed her head. 'And I think you're rather despicable. You can't even be true to her *before* you're married. Maybe your first wife had cause to go off with someone else.'

His jaw jutted dangerously. 'I should put you across my knee for that.'

'You and who else?' she scoffed.

'Don't tempt me!' From the look in his eyes she thought she had better not. And she did feel slightly ashamed to have hit him below the belt. 'Lucky for you I'm feeling forgiving,' he went on. 'I'm determined to bury the hatchet. I expect you to cooperate. Let's go in to dinner.'

Silently she got out of the car and slammed the door. He took her arm and walked her to the cocktail bar. 'You flirt with me unashamedly,' he accused, 'and then you turn on the ice, you Jezebel.'

'It's a game two can play,' she said serenely.

In the red-carpeted lounge she took a seat in one of the deeply cushioned armchairs, crossing her slim legs and glancing around with apparent non-chalance while he ordered drinks. There was a large pedestal of clove carnations, pink roses and white daisies against a white and gold wall, their scent mingling with the faint aroma of alcohol and tobacco.

'This is a super place,' she said, being deter-minedly affable to further the illusion of her in-difference.

'I'm glad something pleases you.'

'I'm not hard to please.' She gave him an angelic smile. 'I'm trying to co-operate.'

He sipped his drink, watching her with narrowed eyes. 'I should think you're being as co-operative as Cleopatra's asp at the moment, Laurel.'

'Then you'll have to watch it, won't you?'

The waiter announced that their table was ready and they went into the restaurant. Keeping the conversation flippant, she gave him a graphic account of the wedding and some of its more amus-ing moments. She also told him about her brother and his plans to go to America. 'I'll probably end up there myself one of these days,' she added airily.

'And what of the immediate future, when you've finished your course at the Riversdale?'

She hadn't given it too much thought, but since she was purporting to be well in control of things, she had to come up with an answer. 'I'll probably look for a sister's post . . . unless I decide to do midder.'

'Perhaps fate will decide things for you,' he said with an odd smile.

'I'm not waiting for fate to take a hand . . . you have to go out there and *make* things happen.'

He threw back his dark head and laughed. 'Too true. As I have said before, there's a wise head on those young shoulders.'

'Oh, don't be so bloody patronising,' she flared.

He laughed even more. 'That's more like the Laurel we know. Simmer down, my dear. You're playing it cool, remember?'

She bit back another angry retort and concentrated on her dinner, sawing at her chicken savagely.

'Don't take it out on the poor fowl. It's not tough.'

Laurel withered him with a glance.

They maintained an uneasy truce for the rest of the meal. He continued to irritate her with veiled hints that he had information she knew nothing of, but she refused to rise to the bait. She realised only too well that her show of indifference cut no ice with him, which was humiliating enough. But neither had she fooled herself. Provoking though he was, there was no denying he drew her like a magnet. Their somewhat stormy journeys together had been fascinating as well as infuriating. But since Bruce was destined to leave the hospital soon, these bitter-sweet rides would no longer be called for.

They continued on their journey and her dejection increased with every passing minute. His attempts at conversation she answered in monosyllables as she faced facts. It wasn't going to be easy to forget him. He aroused feelings within her that she hadn't known she was capable of. Here was a man she could have loved wholeheartedly, if he'd wanted her. But it was a lost cause—because he was going to be married to somebody else.

She had a morbid desire to know if it was Moira Carp who was the lucky one. She couldn't ask outright, so she tried to draw him out by saying, 'I was sorry to hear of Moira's breakdown.'

'Were you? I got the impression you two didn't get on.'

'Oh, we didn't always see eye to eye, but I don't wish her any harm.'

'Moira's a survivor,' he said, casually, and went on to talk of something else, so she was no wiser than before.

It was ten o'clock when he pulled up outside the house. 'Here you are.' He was extraordinarily cheerful. 'I'll get your case for you.' He went round to open up the boot and carried the case to the darkened porch. 'I take it I wouldn't be popular if I were to exercise my privilege again?' he said with a maddening smile.

'Diagnosis correct. Thanks for the lift, and the dinner.' She held out her hand.

He took it in his warm, firm grasp. 'Goodbye, Miss Unflappable,' and he left her.

He had said goodbye, not goodnight. With a deep sigh she let herself into the house. That 'goodbye' had the ring of finality about it. It was as though another door had slammed in her face. Her throat ached with unshed tears. The heaviness in her breast was a physical pain.

No one else was at home, which was another let-down. She carried her case upstairs, took off her glad rags and put on her dressing gown before starting to unpack. For company she switched on her transistor. 'It's not the end of the world if he's married,' came the plaintive singing of a pop star. Laurel sighed again. No, of course it wasn't the end of the world, only it sure as hell felt like it.

She put away her things, thoughts of Bruce and her father, Ingrid and Tom all jumbled up in her mind. She felt isolated from everyone. They all had plans and were going places. Laurel's world had come to an end.

There was still her work, she reminded herself. Concentrating on that would be bound to take her mind off personal matters. And it wouldn't be too soon to start looking at ads in the nursing magazines to see what she could do when her course finished. She squared her shoulders and made a determined effort to snap out of her doldrums. She might even be offered a sister's post at the Riversdale if one came up. With Moira gone and Bruce going that would now be an acceptable solution.

It was ten forty-five when Emma came in. Laurel ran down to greet her, glad of someone to talk to at last.

'I wondered when you'd get back,' said Emma, looking glad to see her. 'Feeling okay now?'

'I'm fine,' said Laurel gaily, 'although weddings

always make me a bit tearful. Daft, isn't it, when they're supposed to be happy occasions. Half of you is glad, and the other half wonders how it will turn out.' She made coffee for them both and carried it into the living-room.

Emma kicked off her shoes and put her feet up on the sofa. 'Well, better get your hankies ready. There'll be another wedding coming up before too long, I shouldn't wonder.'

'Oh? Who's that?'

'Dilys and Andy have got themselves engaged.'

'I'm not surprised,' said Laurel. 'So another free spirit bites the dust.'

'Dear me, you have got post-wedding blues,' laughed Emma. 'She's got a sweet little ring . . . coral and pearls. It belonged to his grandmother. He's going to buy her a proper one when he's in the lolly. There's going to be a gig for them in the doctors' mess next Saturday. How did you get back?' she went on. 'Did your brother bring you?'

'No . . . Bruce.' She told Emma about his plans to join her father's practice. 'And apparently he's getting married soon, too.'

'Must be an epidemic. Well, we're not in danger of catching it yet, are we?'

Laurel made a wry face. 'No. Remember when you flipped your lid over Phil? Bruce said then that love was a source of great unhappiness. Looks like someone's managed to change his mind.'

'Well, he's too dishy to stay on the shelf for ever. I wonder who it is?'

'I haven't a clue,' shrugged Laurel. 'He wasn't forthcoming about it. How's the old firm? I'm really looking forward to getting back in the groove. Funny how you miss the place.'

Emma passed on the latest hospital gossip before they both decided to call it a day.

CHAPTER TEN

GOING on at one o'clock the next day, Laurel received a great welcome from the rest of the staff and slipped back easily into the work of the department. For the time being she still had to face up to working under the same roof as Bruce. She had made up her mind to appear politely unconcerned when they met, although she knew that every minute in his company was going to be fraught with difficulty for her.

As it happened she did not come up against him for the rest of that week. Not that it prevented her from going around like a cat on hot bricks, fearful that she might bump into him. And with every nook and cranny of the department reminding her of their various clashes, it was impossible to keep him out of mind.

In Moira Carp's place temporarily there was the locum, as Dilys had said. Tim Benders was an owlish, bespectacled, rather serious young man with conventionally short mousy hair. He had little sense of humour but was determinedly dedicated. He suited Laurel's present frame of mind very well. She was in no mood for Bob Merrick's flirty ways, or for Andy's subtle jokes for that matter.

She was with Benders in one of the examination rooms, dealing with a middle-aged man who had been brought in unconscious off the street. He'd

173

been having a fit, the police had said, but although the fitting had stopped he had still not recovered consciousness. His skin was sweaty and clammy.

With a puzzled air Dr Benders pushed his glasses up on his nose. 'Well, he's obviously epileptic, but why isn't he coming round? Everything else seems normal as far as I can tell.' He raised the patient's eyelids. 'Pupils okay. No signs of head injury. Pulse on the slow side. Any ideas, Nurse?'

Laurel remembered noticing evidence of puncture marks on his thighs when she had undressed the man, but his normal pupils did not indicate drug abuse. 'He's been injecting himself with something . . . insulin?'

Dr Benders clicked his fingers as the light dawned. 'He's diabetic. I should have spotted that. Very perceptive of you.' He glanced at her with respect. 'Now, is he hyper or hypo? We'd better test.'

He pricked one of the patient's fingers with a sterile needle and squeezed a drop of blood onto the dextrostix which Laurel handed to him. 'Hm . . . blood sugar only two,' he said, watching it register. 'So he's hypo. We'll get some dextrose into him.'

Laurel produced the fluid pack while he inserted the canula into a vein in the patient's arm. Together they set up the intravenous drip and waited for the man's blood-sugar level to rise.

Dr Benders became quite chatty, appreciating the value of his competent assistant. 'Have you been here long, Nurse Swann?'

'Just over five months. I'm more than half-way

through the post-grade A and E course.'

'I should think you're a natural for this work,' he said. 'It needs a cool head.' As she stretched up to adjust the rate of flow of the i.v. drip, he noticed the newish scar on her neck and nodded towards it. 'What have you done there?'

'That was one of the times when my cool deserted me. There was a knife-throwing incident in one of the treatment rooms. I forgot to duck.'

'I heard about that. So it was you, was it?'

She smiled. 'Mm. It all happens at the Riversdale.'

He allowed himself to smile in return. The patient was beginning to come round now, as his blood-sugar rose. 'What's the drill here?' Dr Benders asked, 'Do we get him admitted to be stabilised?'

'I should think so. You'll have to contact the medical registrar, though, to see what he says.'

He went off to telephone while she stayed with the man, talking to him as consciousness returned.

'Hallo, love. Are you beginning to feel a bit better?'

Blinking a little, he gave her a vacant smile. 'What's the matter . . . did I pass out?'

'Yes. You've had a hypo. What's your name?'

'Charlie Dukes.'

'Have you been missing out on some meals, Mr Dukes?'

He nodded. 'The wife's away. Expect I haven't been eating what you might call regular. I've been taking my insulin though.'

'That's the trouble,' Laurel said. 'Too much

insulin and not enough food. We've corrected that, given you some glucose. You're epileptic too, aren't you?'

He looked a little sheepish. 'Yes . . . I don't always remember to take my pills. The wife usually dishes them out to me.'

Dr Benders came back, reporting that the registrar would be down shortly but that beds were at a premium.

'Well, we can always put him in the day-room overnight,' said Laurel. She was thankful that it was a medical case and that it would not be Bruce coming to see the patient. She made out the necessary charts now that Mr Dukes was in a position to give them details and Dr Benders wrote out his case history.

'We'll have to let someone know where you are, Mr Dukes,' Laurel said after making him comfortable in the day ward.

'I'd rather you didn't tell my wife . . . she's gone up North to see her sick dad. I've got a married daughter living nearby . . .'

He gave her the telephone number and Laurel went off to make contact, well satisfied with her morning's work.

Although he took himself rather seriously, Laurel had liked working with Dr Benders. It was a treat not to have to ward off the advances of Bob Merrick, or to be on tenterhooks with Moira Carp, or to be blithe and merry with Andy when she felt anything but.

Her one desire at that moment was to concentrate on the job and to stay out of Bruce's way for as long as he continued to work at the Riversdale.

For the whole of that week Dilys had been wearing a permanently ecstatic expression. Both she and Andy were well-liked and the news of their link-up, spreading like wildfire through the hospital, had been received with general acclaim.

The three girls were sharing an evening together at the house the night before the engagement party, deciding what they would wear and who might be expected to turn up.

'Do you think I'd be all right in my green off-the-shoulder dress?' asked Laurel. 'If I wear a velvet ribbon round my neck the scar won't be too obvious, will it?'

'Don't worry about it,' said Dilys. 'Everyone knows what happened. It's nothing to be ashamed of. Wear it like a badge of honour!'

Laurel wrinkled her nose. 'It's one I'd rather be without. Have you and Andy actually set a date for the wedding?'

'No, not yet. We're going to wait until he's done his Paeds and fixed up a registrar's job somewhere. But I'll probably move to wherever he goes.'

'So it looks like we may all be breaking up soon.' Laurel sighed. 'Sad, isn't it? It's been great while it lasted.'

Dilys was irrepressible. 'Oh, I expect both of you will be finding yourselves blokes before too long. If I know anything about Mike, Em's as good as booked already.'

Emma laughed. 'I'm not rushing into anything. Once bitten, twice shy.'

'At one time that's what Bruce Tyson said,' Laurel remarked.

'At one time I thought he might be struck on *you*,' said Emma.

'Me? We're about as compatible as cat and dog.' Laurel yawned. 'Oh well, I'll have to get some shut-eye if I'm to be hyped up for the party. I'm on first shift tomorrow. G'night, folks.'

She took herself off to bed, but in the darkness she lay awake for some time. The mention of Bruce had brought him vividly back to mind. Had he really met someone who had bowled him over? Or was it to be a marriage of convenience in order to give David a stable home? Certainly someone or something had created a change in him. He had even been prepared to be agreeable towards her on that last journey home. It was she who had been the quarrelsome one, by way of self-preservation.

Drifting into the realms of fancy, she wondered how things might have turned out if Bruce had been attracted to her. If only he had been! In her mind's eye she pictured them both in some pastoral setting, Bruce with his arm around her and David with a lovable pooch, something like Bengy, gambolling ahead of them. But it was a futile exercise escaping into cloud-cuckoo land, she told herself severely. What she had to do was to bury him firmly in the past and waste no more time on pipe-dreams. She was a free agent. Her life was her own. There was a whole world out there, full of people, people who liked her even if he didn't. Anyway, Bruce would no doubt be spending all his free time with the girl of his choice, so he would hardly be likely to show up at the party tomorrow. That at least would give her the opportunity of enjoying it.

It was the usual busy Saturday on A and E. With Sister Maguire on a long weekend, it was Laurel's turn to have responsibility for the smooth running of the department until another senior staff nurse came on duty. There were the usual walking wounded to deal with—people with insect bites, sunburn, cut fingers and sprained ankles; others with stitches for removal and wounds for re-dressing. And there were the usual complaints from the odd impatient individual not prepared to wait his turn.

'When is someone going to see my boy!' one irate father bellowed at Laurel as she approached the next patient in line. 'We've been hanging about here for over an hour. It's not good enough.'

'We always see people in strict rotation,' she explained patiently.

'No you don't. What about that kid you just took in?' he accused. 'We were here before him!'

The child in question had been greatly distressed with an acute attack of asthma. He had needed prompt treatment with a Ventolin nebuliser to help his breathing.

'That was an urgent case. Of course we have to deal with some things immediately.'

She looked at the admission card which the man held. It showed the time they had booked in and they had, in fact, been waiting only thirty minutes, not the length of time the father had said.

The boy had a boil on his neck but it was hardly a matter of life or death. Trying to be tactful, she did not comment on the father's exaggeration. 'We won't keep you waiting any longer than we can help,' she said.

The next patient rolled her eyes sympathetically at Laurel. 'Think you've got four pairs of hands, some people, don't they?'

The afternoon was taken up with a road traffic accident involving multiple fractures, for which they had to call the orthopaedic registrar. There followed a young woman haemorrhaging heavily from a ruptured ectopic pregnancy, which required consultation with the gynaecologist. There were hurried visits to the Path Lab with blood samples for cross-matching and preparations for the emergency life-saving operation which was called for.

Laurel went off duty at five o'clock, half an hour late, but in plenty of time to get ready for the night's festivities. She had always liked her green voile dress with its deep-frilled neckline, and with the velvet band around her neck, the scar wasn't too evident.

Emma looked demure as always, in a fine blue Indian cotton which brought out the softness of her dreamy blue eyes. Dilys was her typical outgoing self in a scarlet chiffon dress with a swinging skirt.

Dilys set off early to meet Andy and to welcome their guests. Laurel and Emma followed a little later, meeting up with Mike and Bob Merrick as they arrived.

In the doctors' mess the lights were dimmed, the

disco deafening and a general air of camaraderie prevailing. After indulging in an energetic session of jiving with Bob, Laurel paused for a long, cool drink, joining Ahmed Singh, Mike and Emma.

With the music once more getting under way, Emma and Mike went off to dance.

'Can I get you another drink, Laurel?' Ahmed asked as he finished his own.

'No, thanks. I'm all right for the moment,' she smiled at him.

He sauntered off in the direction of the bar to replenish his own glass. She caught sight of Tim Benders looking a little lost and was about to go up and talk to him when there was a light tap on her shoulder. Turning, she found herself face to face with Bruce.

Her stomach knotted and her cheeks flamed as his deep blue eyes met hers. He looked so ruggedly handsome, in fawn cord trousers and a brown checked shirt under his cashmere sweater, she caught her breath. 'Oh! Hallo.' She swallowed nervously and stammered, 'I—I'm surprised you could make it. No Tonbridge this weekend?'

He shook his head. 'David has gone to stay with a schoolfriend. They went to the zoo today.' His mouth twitched. 'Well, have you got over your tantrums?'

Laurel clenched her fists and said frostily, 'Only children have tantrums.'

'Exactly.' He suppressed a smile.

She glared at him. 'If you're referring to our journey home, I think I had every right to feel provoked that night.'

He tutted with mock self-reproach. 'I shall have to mend my ways, shan't I?'

What a supreme egoist the man was. 'Too right! You were insufferable.'

'Well, let's see if we can put things right, shall we?' He took the glass from her hand and set it on the table. 'Come with me. I want your opinion on something.'

Him and his male machismo . . . he thought he was irresistible! Well, she would show him that it didn't matter tuppence to her what he did or wanted. 'Ask me now,' she said, standing her ground.

'No. Come along.' He was standing so close to her that she had to look up to him. If she'd had the courage she would have stamped on his foot.

'I'm not going anywhere with you,' she said resolutely.

'Oh yes you are.' He seized her hand. His touch electrified her, but she couldn't create a scene in front of everyone and so she had no option but to allow herself to be drawn to the exit.

The night air fanned her hot cheeks and ruffled the frill of her thin dress. She shivered, and not entirely from cold. This was no way to cut him out of her life. This was just prolonging the agony; another fresh start to be made.

'Here, you'd better put this on.' He peeled off his sweater and placed it around her shoulders, tying the sleeves under her chin. 'Can't have you taking a chill.'

The sweater held his own personal, masculine odour. She felt stupidly euphoric at the warmth left by his body. 'Wh-where are you taking me?' she asked in a tremulous voice.

'Not far. Just to my rooms.'

Oh God, no! This was crazy. 'I—I don't know that I want to come. Is it absolutely necessary?'

'Absolutely.' He continued to walk her, willy-nilly, in the direction of the residents' quarters at the back of the hospital.

'But why should you want my opinion? We hardly ever agree about anything.'

He curbed a smile as he glanced down at her, squeezing her hand. 'Wait and see. There's one thing I think we do agree upon.'

They approached the flat-roofed two-storey block of living units. Bruce pushed open the spring-closing entrance door to let her pass through. Laurel had never been in the residents' quarters before. Now she found herself in a square hall with russet-coloured carpet tiles. A curving staircase led to the upper floor.

'This way.' Bruce prodded her in the direction of the stairs. At the top they went down a side corridor where he unlocked the door to his unit.

'Make yourself comfortable.' He indicated the tweed-covered settee in his living-room and went over to his drinks cabinet. 'Dry Martini?'

'Thank you.' She threw off the sweater and sat down, clasping her knees, her eyes wide with disbelief. She was actually here, alone with Bruce in his room, and at his request. Why, for heaven's sake?

Absently she took in details of the room. It was cluttered and comfortable. Folk-weave curtains

framed the window. Books overflowed from the
wall-shelves. There was a desk high with papers
and journals. A white telephone. A squash racket
in a press stood in one corner and on the small table
by the settee there was a cricket yearbook, similar
to those her father read.

'Well?' she demanded, taking the drink he handed her and setting it down on the table. Her blood
was racing, but she made a great effort to be cool.

He strolled over to his desk, ferreted among a
pile of papers, took up a large envelope and returned to drop it into her lap. Standing in front of
her, hands in his pockets, he said, 'I'd like you to
look at those.'

She withdrew a sheaf of papers from the en-
velope. They were house agents' property sheets.
Laurel glanced up at him with a puzzled frown.
'Well?' she said again.

'Anything there you fancy?'

Her frown deepened. She stared at the papers
and then back at Bruce. 'You're thinking of buying
one?'

'Yes.'

Something inside her snapped. Her anger boiled
over. How dare he expect her to take an interest in
his matrimonial plans just because he was linking
up with her father? This was going too far. 'Why
should my opinion matter?' she snapped, her eyes
flashing. 'You should be consulting your future
bride, not me. I doubt very much whether we have
anything in common.'

She bounced up to leave, but he pushed her
down again and sat beside her. 'Oh, but I'm sure

you have.' Looking into her face, he murmured, 'That *is* who I am consulting.'

Her mouth gaped. She was sure she must have misunderstood what he said. 'Wh-what did you say?'

His lips twitched. 'Don't you recognise a proposal when you hear one?'

Laurel's brain whirled. Her colour came and went. 'A-a proposal of what?' she stammered.

'Of marriage, girl. What else?'

She was dumbstruck. All her alarm bells rang. He was offering her marriage? But why the sudden change of heart? She edged away from him, shaking, as her mind groped for reasons. Perhaps the other girl had turned him down. Perhaps he'd decided that this would be a tidy arrangement. But much as she yearned for him, she could never settle for that kind of marriage, for being second best.

'I—I don't know what you're up to,' she blurted out. 'If this is your idea of a joke, it's in very poor taste.'

His hand dropped around her shoulders and he gave her a little shake. 'Marriage is no joke, Laurel. I've never been more serious in my life. And don't you think it's time we stopped playing games, hmm?'

Her heart was stampeding, thudding in her ears. 'I—I don't know what you mean.'

He eyed her steadily. 'I think you do. Despite the charades we've been playing, I have reason to believe that you wouldn't be opposed to the idea. And don't look at me with those child's eyes, Laurel, or I can't vouch for my self-control.'

She bit her lips. How could he possibly know how she felt about him when she had gone to such lengths to conceal it?

He divined her thoughts. 'How do I know?' Lightly his fingers stroked the scar on her neck. 'Perhaps I should feel indebted to the guy who did this. Some of your ramblings when your defences were down were quite revealing.'

Her cheeks flamed. 'That? I-it was probably utter nonsense,' she protested feebly, feeling exposed. 'People say all sorts of things when they're not in control.'

'Or they lose their inhibitions and give way to their fundamental instincts.' His arm tightened around her.

She swallowed against the lump in her throat, her body trembling. 'I-if you're wanting a tidy arrangement for you and your son, forget it. You can get yourself a housekeeper, like my father did.'

His hand slid under the frill of her dress, stroking her bare shoulders, inflaming her beyond bearing. 'As you say, of course I could. But I don't wish to. I want to marry you.'

Tears threatened to choke her. She fought to keep them back. 'But what about love?' she said shakily. 'Does that enter into it? I-it sounds more like a business proposition.'

'Ah! I'm rather out of practice with the niceties of courting.' He slid off the sofa and went down on one knee in front of her. 'Darling Laurel . . . I love you very much. I have done so for a long time. Please marry me?'

'Oh, get up and don't be a fool,' she said, dashing

a hand across her eyes. She still could not believe him. It seemed like an impossible dream, something that happened to other people, or in fiction.

He sat down beside her again, his intensely blue eyes searching her bewildered face. 'I am a fool . . . a perfect fool where you're concerned. What do I have to do to convince you?'

He did the only sensible thing. He wrapped her in his arms, murmuring, 'Stop fighting me, darling. I know it's what you want . . . it's what we both want.'

She buried her face in his shoulder, feeling powerless to resist him. She didn't want to fight him any longer. She relaxed and gave herself up to the seduction of his caresses.

Much later, as they lay in each other's arms, exchanging the foolish dialogue of lovers, he stroked her hair and said huskily, 'Are you sure you want to take on a chap like me, with a ready-made family? Am I asking too much. You're very young.'

Laurel breathed a sigh of purest pleasure. 'Stop talking like a geriatric. I'm not in my infancy. When did you make up your mind that you loved me?'

'Oh, I knew right from our very first exchange of hostilities in the treatment room that day that if ever I thought of marrying again it would have to be someone sweet, good and gutsy, like you.'

She grinned. 'You haven't always thought me good. Quite the reverse, in fact.'

He dropped a kiss on her nose. 'That was the green-eyed monster talking, girl with eyes like emeralds.'

'You've been in some foul moods,' she accused.

'Uh-huh. And I don't mind telling you, I've had some hefty battles with myself. I thought I'd finished with love. I didn't want to love you. I found it impossible not to. And if it hadn't been for your accident I might have gone on believing it was hopeless for me to win the heart of a bewitching little baggage like you.'

He buried his face against the satin-smoothness of her throat, his lips travelling to the soft rise of her breasts. 'With my body I thee worship,' he whispered.

She cradled his head in her arms, running her fingers through his rich, dark hair. 'What did I say . . . what did I let slip that gave the game away?'

Bruce chuckled and lifted his face to hers again. 'You're surely not asking me to betray the confidences of a patient?'

She could scarcely contain her joy as they kissed. It was incredible to think that he wanted her as much as she wanted him. Suddenly, like a tiny cloud on the horizon, a thought struck her. There had to be a snag. She pulled away, sharply, fright in her eyes. 'Bruce, it can't last, can it? Something's bound to go wrong. It always does when you love people. I mean, it's happened to me, it happened to you, it happened to Emma . . .'

With an indulgent smile he pulled her back to him. 'My darling girl, happiness is now. Not yesterday, or tomorrow. Why deny it for the sake of what may never happen? Once I told myself I would never risk falling in love again. Then I met you and went through hell because I thought you could never care for me. By accident I learned differently. I don't intend to lose you now . . . and I'd like to bet we've a lot of tomorrows to look forward to.'

She was willing to be convinced. She sighed and relaxed and said, dreamily, 'I wonder what my father will say?'

'Oh, he knows all about it, and he's in favour.'

Laurel sat up with a start. 'He knows? You mean, you spoke to him . . . before you asked me?' She put on a show of indignation. 'You've got a nerve.'

'Well, I'm an old-fashioned guy. I like to have the seal of approval.' He silenced her protests with a deep and demanding kiss.

'Do you think David will accept me?' she asked presently.

'The nice lady with the dog? I told you you'd scored there, so there's no need to worry about David.'

'And what about your parents?'

'You must come and meet them as soon as we can arrange it. They won't be able to resist you. Anyway, they happen to think that everything I do is wonderful.'

'Modesty is not your strong point, is it?'

'And you're not too big to be spanked, so watch it,' he warned. 'Any more questions?'

She sighed with happiness. 'I expect I'll think of something later. What about the houses? I haven't even looked through them.'

'You can do that at your leisure. Right now, much as I loathe to break this up, don't you think it's about time we went back to the party?'

'Yes, I suppose so.' She was reluctant to leave the heaven of his arms, to share him with anyone yet.

He rose and drew her to her feet, taking her face between his hands and smothering it with kisses. 'Go and tidy your hair. You look a bit rumpled. There's a comb in the bathroom.'

She went and did as he said, and from the mirror the eyes that stared back at her had never been so bright.

'Shall we spill the beans tonight?' he said when she came back, 'I feel like shouting it from the housetops.'

Laurel considered for a moment, then shook her head. 'I don't think that would be fair, do you? This night belongs to Dilys and Andy. We wouldn't want to steal their thunder.'

He placed his sweater around her shoulders again, tying the sleeves under her chin. 'That's why I love you, you sweet kid.'

'Not so much of the kid, please, if we're to be a partnership,' she said pertly.

His eyes twinkled. 'I'll allow you to be a sleeping partner,' he retorted, 'but otherwise I'm in charge, remember.'

Hand in hand they went out into the night. A million stars lit the black velvet sky as they strolled back to the doctors' mess, just in time to see Dilys and Andy being lifted shoulder-high as someone banged out 'Congratulations' on the piano.

They hugged their secret to themselves, but it was obvious to anyone with half an eye that Laurel Swann and Bruce Tyson were alone in that room full of people; alone in a special rose-coloured world of their own.

Catching sight of them, Emma looked puzzled and glanced at Mike. 'What's going on there, I wonder? She told me he was planning to get married.'

'And no marks for guessing who to,' laughed Mike.